THE LAST GOODBYE

Seaside Sisters Series

KAY LYONS

Kindred Spirits Publishing

Chapter 1

Dominic Dunn hit his turn signal and waited for a family of five to cross the sidewalk before he turned into the Carolina Cove Inn lot and parked, dread filling his stomach. Just the sight of the happy families and tourists wandering the sidewalks, lounging on restaurant patios, and enjoying the lively Saturday night left him angry. He should've ignored the letter. Ignored his next-door neighbor and best friend, ignored his boss and coworkers who said he had to honor Lisa's last request and come here.

"Mister? You gonna get out?"

The boy's voice startled Dominic and he turned to see a kid around eight years old watching him. The salt-air breeze blowing through the open windows of his car brought with it the smell of fried foods from the restaurants nearby, and seagulls squawked as they flew overhead.

"Mister?"

"Yeah," Dominic said, only then realizing he'd pulled into a parking place and was literally sitting there with his foot on the brake as he debated his choices of whether to throw the new car in reverse and floor it to get out of Carolina Cove as quickly as possible… or stay the prepaid two weeks Lisa had booked for him before her death.

"Doesn't look like it. Are you drunk?"

A rough-sounding chuckle left his chest. "Do you get a lot of drunk people here?"

"Sometimes."

"I see. Well, I'm not drunk. Just trying to decide if I want to stay here."

"Oh. You got a reservation?"

Did the kid ever stop asking questions? A memory formed, that of his son, Elijah, at the same age "Yeah, I do."

"Then why don't you wanna stay?"

Dominic glanced at the clock and noted the time. If he left now, he'd add another six hours to his drive from Atlanta. Not how he wanted to spend what was left of the day. Maybe he should spend the night and head back to Atlanta first thing in the morning? "You've convinced me. I guess I will stay."

"I'll show you the way to the office."

"Do your parents know you're out here near the street? You're awfully young to be wandering about on your own."

The kid's shoulders squared and he lifted his chin to a defiant angle.

"I'm almost ten."

He looked younger, maybe because of his small stature. "Well, almost ten or not, there are a lot of strangers milling around, and it's not safe for kids these days. Are you visiting?" He sounded like an old man talking about "the good old days" but it was true. What kind of parent just let their kid wander the streets in a beach town full of people, some of whom probably waited on the opportunity to grab a kid and head out of town?

"No. I live here. You coming or not?"

The kid had spunk, Dominic had to give him that.

He rolled up the windows of the Porsche 911, killing the powerful engine with another press of a button. He felt a little conspicuous driving the flashy car, but he had to admit he loved the power. Just like Lisa knew he would.

He opened the door and climbed out of the low vehicle, yet another thing to get used to after driving a family-friendly SUV for so many years.

"Wow. You're tall. My mom is too. I hope I'm tall when I grow up."

Dominic locked the car and fell into step behind the boy. "I see the sign for the office. You can head home if you like."

"No. I need to check in anyway." The kid turned around and walked backward, rolling his eyes in classic kid fashion. "Or my mom will freak out and call the police again."

Again? "Does that happen a lot?"

"Her calling the police or freaking out?"

"Take your pick."

"Yeah."

Yeah to… both? Dom bit back another chuckle. Given the kid's intrepid personality, he probably kept his mom busy.

The kid flipped face-forward and Dom watched as

the boy ran up the two steps leading to the office. He yanked open the door.

"Mom! Reservation!"

Dom noted the wide southern porch with its rocking chairs and a few chairs and tables before he followed the kid inside, well able to see why Lisa had liked the inn so much if the porch and office interior were anything by which to judge. It was her style of decorating. Beachy but understated.

The office walls were a soft gray with blue and sand-colored accents. There was a comfortable-looking couch and chair in the waiting area, a rope swing hanging from the ceiling in front of a painted mural of the beach and ocean behind, and on the opposite side, a coffee bar, popcorn machine, and snack area with a couple of parlor-type tables and chairs.

"Mom!"

"Samuel, how many times have I told you? No yelling. Inside voice," a woman stated as she appeared from a hallway behind the chest-high desk.

Dominic stilled, uncomfortable with the stomach-punching fact he found her beautiful. He'd guess her age to be early to mid-thirties, tall like her son said, at around five eight. Her auburn hair was scooped back and held at her nape, but curly tendrils framed her face and highlighted striking eyes that matched the blue of the ocean painting behind the check-in area.

"But, Mom, you have a reservation and sometimes don't hear me."

"A— Oh," she said, locking gazes with Dominic. "Sorry about that. Welcome to Carolina Cove Inn. I'm Ireland Cohen, the manager."

He forced himself to focus on her name rather than her beauty. "Ireland? Like the country?"

"Yes."

"Unusual name."

"Unusual family," she said by way of explanation. She flashed them both a smile. "I hope I didn't keep you waiting too long?"

"Not at all. Samuel kept me company."

"Mom, you should see his cool car! I'll bet it goes really fast. Does it?"

"It does."

"Maybe you'll take me for a ride sometime?"

"Samuel."

"I'm leaving tomorrow."

"Oh."

"And even if he wasn't, Samuel, that's not something you ask our guests. We've talked about this, remember?" the boy's mother said while sliding her son a stern glare.

"Yes, ma'am."

Samuel glanced at Dominic and rolled his eyes, and yet again Dom found himself stifling a chuckle. And wondering at the last time he'd laughed so much in such a short span of time. "Tough break, kid."

"Let's get you checked in. Name?"

"Dominic Dunn."

"Domin—"

His name ended with a gasp and Ireland's eyes filled with tears. She blinked rapidly and managed to keep them from falling, but in that instant, he knew she recognized him—and knew his reason for being there.

Chapter 2

Ireland bit her tongue in an attempt to pull herself together. She blamed her emotional reaction on the stress of the day, but she knew the tears were really the raw reality of life. "I'm sorry. My night manager had an emergency and I-I just got here. I hadn't had a chance to look at the reservation list or I would've— I-I'm so, so sorry for your loss."

Dominic Dunn stood before her looking every bit the sad, weary man Lisa had claimed he would be. Tall, with a bit of silver starting to shine at his temples due to the overhead lights, he looked physically fit but worn, the lines around his eyes and forehead deep despite a year's distance from the tragedy of Lisa's death.

A copy of Lisa Dunn's obituary had been sent to her by the friend who had traveled with Lisa to Carolina Cove after Lisa's diagnosis. The news was both sad and informative because it meant Lisa's plan for her beloved husband was going into play. And now… now Dominic Dunn stood before her, six foot plus of mourning male, and Ireland felt sadness and anger and jealousy, even envy, all balled up in a horrible mix.

"Thank you. I take it you know whatever arrangements Lisa made?"

His words dragged her out of the quagmire of her mind, and she nodded and cleared her throat of the emotional lump.

That she did. On the last day of her stay, Lisa had come to Ireland and asked to schedule a reservation for one year after her death. Lisa had wanted to do something for her husband like what she'd seen in a movie, where the dying husband planned surprises for his wife to help her recover from his passing. Lisa's friend would inform Ireland of Lisa's passing and that would set the clock, so to speak. She'd paid in advance. And left a letter to be given to her husband after his stay was completed.

"Mom? What's wrong? You look weird."

She cleared her throat again and gave Samuel a look she hoped would silence him, at least momentarily. "Samuel, be still. Um… Let me just…" She quickly pulled up the reservation and got Dominic checked in, swiping key cards for his use along with printing a parking sheet for his car. "You're in the suite. Room three hundred. There's an elevator located right there," she said, pointing it out, "or you can take the stairs outside. The suite has a sitting area, small kitchenette, and large balcony. This is a parking confirmation," she said, holding up the paper. "Just place the notice on your dash when you're here so you don't get towed. Unfortunately parking is an issue this time of year and people try to take advantage."

"No problem."

"You have coffee in your room, but we also have it here, as you can see, as well as snacks you can purchase. If you want something a little more substantial, you can order in or take the hallway to the right of your door and go to the pier house. Just don't forget your key card to get back into the door because otherwise you'll have to come all the way around and enter here through the office, which closes at ten p.m. The pier house is open twenty-four hours, and I've included a list of local restaurants and our favorite coffee shop."

"My aunt London owns the coffee shop," Samuel said.

"Ireland and London?"

"Unusual family," Ireland repeated, a smile replacing some of the sadness and anger she'd felt since learning his identity. "All of my sisters were named after the place they were conceived."

Despite the fatigue he wore like his travel-wrinkled clothes, Dominic smiled. He was handsome when he smiled.

"How many sisters?"

"There are five of us in all."

He whistled softly. "Our two were a handful. I can't imagine five. What are their names?"

"Ireland, London, Holland, Frankie—France—and Carolina," Samuel quickly said, ticking off their names on his fingers. "Cool, huh?"

Dominic pierced her with his dark-eyed gaze, his amusement crinkling the crow's feet around his eyes. "Military family or world travelers?"

"Military," Samuel said as he swiped a package of peanut butter crackers from the display. "My grandpa is a colonel."

"A retired colonel, and I saw that," she said.

"I'm hungry."

"You're always hungry but those are for the guests. Your snack is in the back."

"Hand me a couple of those, would you, Samuel?"

Samuel did as Dominic requested, and he placed them on the counter.

"How much?"

"Two dollars." Dominic pulled several ones from his wallet to give to her before handing one of the packages to her son. "Oh, you don't have to—"

"Thanks! These'ns are my favorite."

"You're welcome, and they're mine, too. Thanks for showing me the way to the office."

Knowing she'd look bad to insist Samuel give the treat back, she filled a small bag with the parking notice, check-in information, local events and times, and general information and handed it to Dominic across the counter. "Thank you—for the snack. And welcome to the Inn—for however long you decide to stay with us."

Dominic took the bag from the counter and added the package of crackers before heading out of the door. She watched him go and waited several seconds after the door shut before rounding the desk and looking out the window.

"Can I play video games *now?*"

Her eyebrows rose when she spotted the "cool car" Samuel had mentioned. That definitely qualified as a cool car, but she could only imagine the cost. Her eleven-year-old Honda might look a little rough, but she liked not having a car payment. Hilda the Honda had kept her safe all this time, and she was grateful to have such a reliable vehicle.

"Mom?"

"Yeah."

"I can? Yesss!"

"Wait, what?" She glanced at Samuel over her shoulder. "I said yes because you said my name. What did you ask?"

"If I can play video games now."

"First tell me why you left baseball practice early. I thought today was the party? Isn't that why I sent drinks?"

Samuel lifted his bony shoulder in a shrug. "It was boring."

"You say Aunt London's coffeehouse is boring, but you spent most of the day there."

"It is but it's not as boring."

"Sammy, if something is going on, you can tell me. Did something happen at practice?"

"No."

"Then why did you leave?"

"I just wanted to. And Aunt London said she likes me helping her at the coffee shop."

"I'm sure she does."

"So can I go play now?"

She crossed her arms over her front and nodded, knowing her son held something back but unsure as to how to get him to talk about it. Talking wasn't something Samuel shied away from, but talking about his feelings? That was another story. Maybe she should call the coach tomorrow and just… check in?

With Samuel in the back room, her gaze returned to the busy streets of Carolina Cove and the parking lot outside. Sammy had gotten out of school for the summer last week, and the tourist season had hit like a color-blasted, flip-flop-wearing bomb had gone off, filling the otherwise small town with crowds.

Dominic finished placing the parking sheet beneath his windshield and now removed a carry-on suitcase. Once the car was locked, however, he simply stood there, bag in hand, and stared up, either at the upper floors of the inn or the sky. She wasn't sure which. But his expression…

Oh, she knew that look. She'd *felt* that look. Recognized the pose because she'd done much the same the day she'd packed her car and Samuel and showed up on her parents' doorstep, heartbroken, reeling, and as lost as Dominic looked right now.

She hugged her arms tighter around her front and tried to pretend it was because of the air conditioning blowing over her.

Life was hard. Hurt was deep. Death inevitable.

But she'd still argue the death of a spouse was easier to accept than having the man she'd loved, the man who'd promised her a lifetime of love, make the conscious decision to rip her heart out because of another woman.

Chapter 3

Early the next morning, Dominic tossed his Dopp kit into his bag and zipped it closed. He grabbed the handle to lift it from the bed only to pause. Lisa had put a lot of thought and love into planning this trip, and after getting some much-needed sleep, he felt bad about cutting it short. But who wanted to go on a beach vacation alone? Had she thought of that? When Lisa had set the trip up, she'd been there with her best friend from grade school. She'd had someone to do all of the things she'd mentioned doing in the letter whereas he… didn't.

He groaned aloud and lowered his chin to his chest. The least he could do was take a quick look around instead of loading up and heading out before the summer traffic thickened as vacation weeks ended while others began.

His stomach growled loudly.

He'd made do with the crackers purchased for himself and Samuel and the remainder of a bottle of water bought at his last gas stop before the bridge into Wilmington. Now his belly ached with hunger, and something about being in this place Lisa had loved so much made him want to go out and explore a bit to find out why. Walk until he found the peace she'd discovered here after her prognosis had changed from bad to terminal.

He turned and grabbed his key card from atop the dresser where he'd left it last night. Food. A walk. Then he'd leave.

Outside, humidity saturated the air in a taste of what the day had in store, but the sun was shining and it looked to be beautiful.

He glanced over the open walkway to the inn's office below, his gaze lingering on the entry door. The manager's teary response to his identity as Lisa's husband had humbled him, but it wasn't the first time someone had shown that reaction. Lisa had that kind of an impact on people. On him. And not a day went by that he didn't ask himself why her and not him. Why her at all?

Not liking the endless spiral his mind was taking, he shoved himself away from the weathered railing and headed toward the door at the end of the long walkway. Quite a few people walked or jogged the streets, along with fishermen pulling carts of supplies behind as they headed toward the pier house.

Dominic pushed through the door to the stairs on the other side, and a minute later, he entered the pier house behind one of the fishermen.

Despite the early hour, a few kids and adults played billiards and video games in the far-right corner of the large building. Parlor tables like those in the inn's office were scattered in the middle around a walk-up food-order area, and T-shirts and knickknack gifts were stacked floor to ceiling everywhere in between. On his left were more items for sale, and ahead of him was the checkout counter, which also doubled as an ice cream bar. Signs posted the prices for fishing from the pier, rules, and answers to what he assumed were all of the other frequently asked questions.

Dominic made his way over to the food-order counter and got a breakfast burrito and coffee to go.

"Hi."

He turned and found Samuel staring up at him, looking bright-eyed and raring to go. "Hey. Figured you'd be sleeping in this morning."

"Hey, Sammy. I have your order ready. Gimme a sec, okay, hon?" the waitress said as she bagged another order.

"Okay."

"Do you have big plans for the day?"

"If it doesn't rain, we might go fishing later after church."

"That sounds like fun."

He shrugged and Dominic followed Samuel's gaze over to where the kids played the machines with their fathers. An uneasy feeling filled his gut, but Dominic shied away from asking the obvious. Samuel's father's whereabouts were none of Dominic's business.

"Here you go, sir. Sorry about the wait."

"No problem." He'd already paid and tipped the waitress. "I thought I might eat on the pier," he said to Samuel to draw the kid's attention away from the corner. "Any advice on the best seat?"

"Nah. They're all good. Just keep your food covered up or the birds will try to get it."

"Good advice."

"Here you go, Sam. Enjoy. And tell your mama I said hi."

"I will. Thank you, Miss Lori."

"You're welcome, hon. Have fun."

"I like eating on the pier the best, but my mom likes to eat on the swings," he said, continuing their conversation.

"I see. Well, maybe she'll surprise you today."

Once again Samuel's gaze was on the kids in the far corner, and Dominic noted Sam made eye contact with one of them before Sam stepped back behind Dominic like he tried to hide. "Friends of yours?"

"They go to my school. I gotta go."

Samuel gripped his food bag and headed toward the entrance. Dominic stood there a long moment. The door to the pier was in the opposite direction of the one Samuel had taken, but maybe he should take a peek outside and make sure Samuel made it to his mom okay? The kid had seemed upset, but the reason why could be as varied as the items for sale in the pier house.

His kids were grown. Hallie was eighteen and studying abroad for the summer. Elijah had just turned twenty and was presently working an internship at a law firm in New York. It was one of the things he was grateful for with Lisa's passing, that their children weren't small and he wasn't faced with raising them alone. It had been hard enough handling her passing with them as young adults, but they'd managed. Somehow.

Which made him wonder… What had happened to Samuel's dad?

Back outside, the call of the birds and sound of crashing waves added to the music coming from the pavilion nearby. While he'd been inside, several men had begun setting up chairs, a sound system, and instruments.

Several feet outside of the entrance, Samuel stood, head down, food bag gripped tight in his hand. "You okay, buddy?"

Samuel straightened his shoulders at the sound of Dominic's query and nodded, but the sniffle gave him away.

"Yeah. My mom's waiting for me. Bye."

Dominic watched as Samuel walked away, feet dragging and looking as downcast as he had inside when he'd spotted his friends and their dads. Dominic tracked Samuel's slow trek to where his mother sat, the sight tugging Dominic's heartstrings until he gave in to the invisible push he felt shoving him in their direction.

Chapter 4

Ireland had a mouthful of omelet wrap when Dominic Dunn approached and asked to join them. Short of breaking her no-talking-with-your-mouth-full rule, which Samuel would no doubt point out, she simply nodded and waved a hand for Dominic to take a seat along the four-foot-high railings separating the board-walk swings from the dunes.

"Thanks."

"You wanna go to church with us?"

Dominic had barely taken a seat when Samuel posed that question, and she noticed that Dominic paused as though he fought the urge to get right back up. "Sorry. Ignore him. I mean, you're welcome to join us, of course, but please don't feel pressured. Samuel, eat your sandwich and leave Mr. Dunn alone."

Samuel looked saddened by the order, and her heart broke a little more. She wasn't oblivious. She'd seen Sammy wipe his eyes after leaving the pier house, and it wasn't but a few seconds later when the Gibson brothers and their father and uncle left the interior of the building for the pier's T. It didn't take a genius to figure out her son was hurting, but she was powerless to help him. Not in the way he wanted and needed.

Sammy craved male companionship, but with her dad on vacation and her sisters each single, Sammy was surrounded by females who tended to baby him instead of allowing him to be a boy, herself included.

Samuel watched his peers on the pier, but every now and again, he'd manage to get a bite in and chew. He ate by rote but showed little interest in his breakfast, the corners of his mouth pulling hard toward the ground.

"Thanks for the invitation but… I plan to check out once I take a quick look around."

"But—"

"*But* we understand, don't we, Samuel? After all, not many people go to church when on vacation. It's a beautiful day to explore, too."

"I didn't get a chance to look at the information you put in the bag last night. Do you have suggestions?"

"Well, there's Fort Fisher, the aquarium, and the beach, of course. Lots of little shops and restaurants here, and in Carolina Beach. Wilmington is full of things to do, too. Did you have something specific in mind?"

"No. Not really."

Because he was so not interested in being here, she mused. The good mood she'd gotten up with this morning quickly dissipated in the face of Samuel's upset and Dominic's sorrow due to his wife's passing.

What would it be like to be loved like that? To be mourned like that? Dominic was young, in his early forties at most, but it was obvious he'd loved Lisa dearly and that… That kind of love was precious. And rare.

Over the last couple of years, she'd learned the signs. Signs she hadn't been able to see in herself and Rich at the time, but recognized in so many of the couples who came and went from the inn. The detachment and distance forming because of life and busyness, the lack of communication, and how so many spent more time staring at their phones than interacting with their families.

She plucked at the paper wrap around her sandwich, lost to memories of her own and wishing she could go back to bed and start the day over again.

They ate in silence for a few minutes, the music from the pavilion, crashing waves, and wind-carried voices filling the void.

"Lisa told me about going to the beachside church service. Said she'd attended when she was here."

Ireland was thankful for the dark sunglasses she wore because they allowed her to stare at Dominic's strong profile as he took in the preparations for the service. "She did."

It was a memory Ireland would cherish of the woman who'd become her friend. She could close her eyes and picture Lisa standing in the pavilion, hands lifted, eyes closed, and head tilted back, singing praise even though she'd just received the worst news of her life.

The memory brought a wave of sadness and clarity, creating a lump in her throat. Things might be difficult for her and Samuel but they could always be worse, and she needed to remember that.

"Since I'm not planning to stay for the entire trip as she planned, maybe that's what I should do. Go in her honor."

She wasn't sure if Dominic expected an answer from her or not, but when she opened her mouth to speak, she found her voice nonexistent thanks to the lump of emotion in her throat.

"You should."

"Samuel." After Dominic had disappeared from view with his suitcase, she'd gone in to check on Samuel and had a brief talk with her son about leaving Dominic alone due to his reasons for being there. In typical kid fashion, however, Samuel was of the opinion Dominic would want company rather than to be on vacation alone.

Clearly a reminder was in order.

Dominic laughed and shook his head as though thoroughly amused by Samuel rather than offended.

"It's okay. And you said after church you were fishing, right?" Dominic asked Samuel.

"Oh, I don't know—"

"Mooom, it's Sunday. We always fish on Sunday."

"Samuel," she said, her tone one of warning.

"Well, we do."

"Sometimes," she countered. "And sometimes we have to work in order to pay for the things that we want. Remember?"

Samuel inhaled deeply and released a gusty sigh. "Mom says I gotta work at the inn and the coffee shop and my aunt Frankie's garage if I want the new Mario game."

"Ahh, that's a good rule. Your mom's right, buddy. My wife and I had a rule that if our kids asked for something that wasn't for a birthday or Christmas gift, they had to earn the money to get it. You value something more that way."

"Is that still the rule since your wife died?"

"Oh, my— *Samuel.* I am so sorry, Mr. Dunn—"

"Call me Dominic. Please. And it's okay. It's a legitimate question, and, yes, it's still the rule. My daughter is a good example, actually. She wanted very badly to study abroad, but after a poor first semester her last year of high school because of her mom's death, she had to work extra hard to get her grades back up to qualify for the program, and get sponsors to help her go. Now she's there and really enjoying it."

"Couldn't you have paid for her to go?"

Dominic nodded. "I could have, and I did help quite a bit. But she was responsible for her grades, and that was the most important thing to attend to, so… she had to do her part if she wanted to go with her friends. You'll find that once you do your part, the other things tend to fall into place."

"Finish your breakfast, Samuel. It's almost time," she said, wadding up the paper wrapper from her sandwich and tossing it into the bag.

"So do you mind? If I join you for church?"

She was startled by the question, maybe a little more than she ought to be. "Not at all. It's come as you are. Everyone is welcome."

"Even dogs," Samuel said.

"Really?"

"Yeah. There used to be a dog who prayed."

"Um, Samuel, maybe—"

"But she died."

Ireland winced.

"I see," Dominic murmured. "Well, I hate to hear that."

Samuel nodded. "Yeah. It was sad. I'm sorry your wife died."

"Thank you, Samuel. I appreciate you saying that."

"Sammy, baby, it's time to finish up and let Mr. Dunn eat, okay?"

"Okay. But… if I promise to get my work done later, before I go to bed, maybe Mr. Dunn could take me fishing? Please?"

Ireland was in the process of taking a drink of her coffee when Samuel posed the question. She swallowed wrong with the shock of it and coughed repeatedly, the swing where she sat shaking with her movements.

"You okay?"

Eyes watering, she waved a hand in front of her face but couldn't get a decent breath. "Samuel." *Cough.* "I'm sure—" *Cough.* "Mr. Dunn is—" *Cough, cough, cough.* "Busy," she finished with a gasp.

"Oh."

"It's true, Samuel. If I'm going home, I need to get on the road as soon as the service is over."

"But you said you were gonna look around. Can't you stay a little longer? Grandpa usually takes me but he's gone, and Mom sucks at it. Please?"

Ireland sounded like a barking seal and people stared at her as they passed.

Dominic stood and gently pounded on her back. "Are you okay?" he asked her again.

As though finally realizing she sat there and literally struggled to breathe, Samuel's attention focused on her. "Mom?"

She managed to get herself under control and removed her sunglasses to wipe the tears from her eyes, unable to do more than nod. Of all things for Samuel to do. Hadn't her talk with him last night done *any* good?

"Samuel, take this and go buy your mom some water."

"No. No, I'm fine. Really." She coughed some more, trying hard to stop but unable to completely. "I'm fine."

"Are you sure?"

"Yes. *A-hem*. Hmm-mmm." She had to clear her throat a few more times, but thankfully her eyes had stopped watering, allowing her to replace the sunglasses and put some distance between her and Dominic's compelling gaze. "Wrong pipe," she said.

"So can we go fishing after church? Just for a little while? Please, Mom? Please, Mr. Dunn?"

Dominic glanced at Samuel before turning his head toward the pavilion and then back at her.

"If your mom says it's okay, it's fine with me." To her, Dominic said, "Actually, fishing was one of the things Lisa suggested I do while I'm here so… I'd love to join you. That is, if you don't mind me tagging along?"

Chapter 5

An hour after the church service, Dominic stared over the railing of the pier at the sunlight glistening off of the water, the minister's sermon on forgiveness spiraling through his head once again.

He'd done all he could to help and support Lisa, care for her, but he couldn't deny there was a part of himself that would always wonder if there wasn't something more that could've been done. If he could've found another doctor, another treatment. Just… more.

"I'm sorry Samuel guilted you into changing your plans."

Ireland's low murmur got carried away on the wind, and he turned to see her focused on the waves down below them. Samuel stood a few feet away, jerking his line and reeling it in yet again in typical impatient-kid fashion. "It's okay. I apologize for changing my plans again. I hope it doesn't mess with your reservations."

"Not at all. You've got the suite for the next two weeks. It's yours whether you stay or go. Lisa wanted to make sure, if you changed your mind, that you could come back to it."

Why? Why had Lisa done that? The car? The trip? What was the point? "Did she say anything to you? When she set this up? Tell you why?"

They'd returned to the inn long enough to get fishing supplies, hats, and sunscreen, and now Ireland's long auburn hair draped over her shoulder in a thick braid. She wore a tank top and shorts with a turquoise ball cap that read *Mermaid Hair Don't Care* and the same pair of sunglasses from earlier that hid her eyes from him.

"Not really. I remember her saying she knew you'd mourn. And she wanted to do something to help."

"That's all she said?"

"I mean, I have my own theories b—"

"Which are?"

She faced the water, head tilted to one side. "A lot of times, people come here when they feel… lost. I mean, it is land's end, like the sign back there says. So, they stare at the ocean and… something about the sounds and the smells seem to help people come to terms with whatever it is that's happened and, after a while, find acceptance."

Acceptance. Not healing. Lisa had returned from the trip calmer than before she'd gone. She didn't cry as much or as often, smiled more. Seemed happy despite the fact her body was slowly killing her.

He wasn't sure anything could ever give him acceptance for that. "You said you and your sisters are named for where you were conceived. And your parents and at least one sister are around, from what I've gleaned from conversation. Have you always lived here with them once your father returned stateside or…?"

She inhaled and braced her flip-flopped feet on the lower rung of the railing. "Sort of. I moved away after I got married, but Sammy and I moved back two years ago…after my ex and I divorced."

"I see. I'm sorry about that."

"Me, too."

"You didn't want a divorce?"

"Not in the beginning. I fought it with every breath. But when it became obvious staying together just wasn't an option anymore, I"—a huff of a laugh left her chest—"came to the beach to stare at the ocean and wound up returning to stay."

"Can't beat the view."

"Got that right. There's just something about it, isn't there?"

He'd never thought of the ocean or beach as anything more than a vacation destination, but sitting there for the last hour listening to the waves and birds and laughter of vacationers… Well, it was nice. Even though he was alone.

Lisa had forced this trip on him because she'd known he wouldn't go anywhere other than on business trips, where he'd stay in his room and work after getting back from meetings or workshops. But in her letter, she'd mentioned wanting him to remember the years before responsibilities and long hours had overtaken his leisure time. Remember when he'd fished and driven a fast car and enjoyed the simple things in life.

He shifted on the backless bench and leaned forward, coming to terms with his thoughts and the gift Lisa had bestowed.

Life. Her letter had reminded him that he was living for them both now.

"Sorry. Sammy never lasts very long out here when it's just me, so I stopped carting the chairs and drinks and all of the stuff people usually bring. I should've taken into consideration the fact there's another guy here. I'll make a run into the pier house and get us something to drink."

She plopped her feet down onto the wood planks of the pier, but before she stood, he asked, "Where's Samuel's dad?"

Had he not been looking down, he would've missed the sight of her hands tightening on the bench where they sat.

"Rich is with his new family. He called and came to see Samuel the first few months after we separated, but we haven't... heard from him since the new baby was born six months into our separation."

Her voice had lowered, but whether it was for the sharing of private information or because of the anger in her tone, he wasn't sure. "So he's nearby?"

"Charlotte. Close enough to see his son but not enough to make the effort." She shoved herself up off of the bench. "I'm going to go get those drinks. Sammy? Stay put. I'll be right back."

"Okay, Mom."

Ireland walked away and Dom stood when he saw Samuel reel in the last of his line. Casting off the close confines of the pier meant keeping an eye out for people passing by who were more aware of the view than the possibility of being snagged by a hook.

A large pelican landed not far from where they stood.

"Hey, Pete."

"I take it you know him?" Dominic was nearly as

fascinated by the large bird as the pelican seemed to be with him. Pete blinked his beady eyes and opened his beak, spreading his wings.

"Yeah, he's my friend. He does that so I'll feed him some bait."

"Ah." Dominic watched as Samuel dug into their supply and found a few choice morsels. Sam tossed them toward Pete, who caught them with practiced ease. "Looks like he's used to getting fed."

"Lots of people know Pete. My mom doesn't like talking about my dad."

The change in topic left Dom a little behind. "You heard that, huh?"

"Yeah. Catch it, Pete!" Sam tossed another piece of fish, and the pelican caught it and tilted his head back and worked to get it down. "Mom tries to do man stuff with me because my dad isn't around, but my grandpa is better at it."

"Is that so?"

"You're pretty good, too."

Dominic laughed. "Well, thanks for the compliment."

"You ever play baseball?"

"Yeah, all through school. I coached my son's Little League team for a few years, too. Why do you ask?"

Samuel shrugged. "No reason."

"You sure about that?"

Pete the Pelican saw bigger fish across the pier and took flight, flapping his wings and doing the same motions as he had when he'd first landed by them. People stopped to take photos.

Samuel turned back to where he'd leaned his fishing pole and baited his hook.

"My grandpa was going to help me learn how to throw a slider, but then he had to take my grandma on a trip for their anniversary since it was a big number."

"A big number, huh? Do you know how many?"

"Forty, I think. I heard my mom tell Aunt Frankie it was a big deal."

"Being married that long is a big deal. Do they own the inn where your mom works?" He hated to seek information from a child, but they had to talk about something until his mom returned.

"Yeah. They're kinda retired but not. My mom says grandpa will never retire because he'd get bored and he likes talking to the fishermen too much. Grandma says he likes looking at the girls on the beach, though."

Dominic chuckled, sure it was probably a little of both. He could see where a man used to traveling and being around people all day would find retirement a drastic change. And the view was a bonus for any red-blooded male. "So you were asking me about baseball because you want to learn how to throw a good slider?"

"Yeah."

"Did you ask your coach?" He looked around to make sure the area was clear when Samuel brought the pole back to cast. With a fling of the rod, the bait went flying, and Dom knew if the kid could throw like he cast, he was a decent player for his age.

"Yeah, but... Never mind. You won't be here anyways."

"You know, it wouldn't take me long to teach you how to throw a good slider."

Samuel's expression made the change in plans worth the unease he felt at lingering in Carolina Cove and possibly taking advantage of the prepaid stay. The kid's face lit up, and he held the rod with one hand while pulling the other fist back in a boyish *Yessss!*

"Well, what's got you so happy? Did you catch something?" Ireland asked.

"No. But Dominic is going to stay longer. Isn't that great, Mom?"

Chapter 6

"Will you stop worrying? They're fine," London said as she set a latte in front of Ireland. "Frankie can see them on the field from her garage, and she's keeping a sharp eye on them."

"I know. And if I had even an inkling that Dominic Dunn wasn't the man Lisa claimed him to be, my son would not be hanging out with him. But you don't have kids. The worry never ends."

"Yeah, well, I may not have kids but I get worrying about weirdos and pervs these days. You Googled, right?"

"Of course."

"So there you go. You know Frankie can and will take him down if she sees anything weird. And if you're that worried, you could walk down there and watch."

She could. But Samuel had made a point of saying it was a "guy trip," and she knew he needed the time without his mom hanging around. Knowing that didn't make doing it any easier to stomach though. "I know. It's just… I feel bad. The man isn't here to fish with my kid or teach him how to throw a ball."

"Stop worrying. He obviously doesn't mind or he wouldn't have agreed. Besides, he's here alone, so maybe it's a good distraction from why, you know?"

"Yeah, I guess." Ireland released a low groan and decided a change in subject was in order. "You haven't stopped glaring at the door. What's up with that?" She watched as her younger-by-two-years sister shrugged. "Uh-uh. Not buying it. Spill."

"Fine. Right before you walked in, I heard that the hurricane may be changing course."

They'd had a few quiet years, but ever since the hurricane last year, London had been more weather-conscious, no doubt due to the weather's impact on her business. "It'll be okay. It's still waaaay out there, which means it could change course a half-dozen times before making landfall."

London inhaled and sighed. "You're right."

Ireland glanced around the coffee shop, taking in the wide array of offerings London displayed in an attempt to make her sales quota and lure in customers. In addition to coffee, ice cream, T-shirts, and books, the shop sold trinkets and postcards and locally made wares. "Everything changes when you own a business *and* live here, doesn't it?"

"Got to pay the price to live in paradise, right? So is he cute?"

"Who?"

"Seriously? Dominic Dunn, that's who. With a name like that he has to be cute. Is he?"

"He's… yeah. Yeah."

"That's it? Two yeahs and a shrug?"

"That's it." Because what could she say? Lisa's husband *was* handsome.

"You kill me."

"What do you expect? The man is a guest at the inn, a widower mourning a sweet friend—"

"The sweet friend who planned this whole weird thing why?"

Good question. "I'm not sure. He asked me about it today, too. If I knew why. It *is* weird, right? I mean, yeah, there was a whole movie based on doing this kind of thing, and it was great, but it was *fiction*. This is real life. Who plans a trip for the one left behind a year later? Lisa was a wonderful person, but I don't understand her thinking then or now. I mean, I don't know how I'd feel about it. It has to be painful. A reminder of everything lost because she's not here to enjoy it with him."

"Maybe this is her goodbye gift?"

"She's gone, Londy. She said goodbye a year ago."

"Yeah, but *may*be this is her last goodbye? As in, she planned this trip for him to one of her favorite places and she's going to tell him to move on. She left a letter for you to give him when he leaves, right?"

Ireland glanced around them even though they were the only two people at the bar. "Shhh. That's a *secret*. I shouldn't have told you that. I was just so blown away at the time when she gave me the letter and left to go home that I had to tell someone."

"And I've kept the secret. What you *shouldn't* have told me is where you put the letter for safekeeping. Do you know how badly I've wanted to steam it open and read it and the restraint it's taken not to?"

"Note to self: move the letter," Ireland muttered as she lifted her coffee for a sip.

"Mmm. Might be wise, especially considering he's actually here now and time is running out to know what it says."

"Stop it. Can we talk about something else?"

"Why? Come on, he's obviously a decent guy if he's up for church, fishing, and teaching your kid a baseball thing."

"He might be but facts are facts—he's just visiting, so it doesn't matter. Plus, it could also be for show. You remember how Rich was always pretending to be such a good guy? He went to church, played dad to Sam, and seemed like such a great person. But when it came down to it, he wasn't what he presented himself to be."

"You can't let that loser keep you from someone new, though."

"I'm not."

"Aren't you?"

"All I'm saying is I don't trust my judgment anymore. And, again, Dominic is a guest, who is now leaving tomorrow instead of today thanks to my son's big blue eyes and request for help. He's not a local who'll be sticking around when the season is over, and even if he was, there's the obvious fact he is still mourning. The man's heart is broken. Anyone can see that."

"Well, I actually wasn't referring to Dominic Dunn when I said that about someone new, but it's interesting that your mind automatically went there." London waggled her eyebrows up and down. "Maybe what Dominic needs is someone to heal the pieces, and who better to do that than someone who knows what it's like to have a broken heart?"

"You never give up, do you?"

"Just being straight with you." London leaned against the counter and tapped her nails against the polished surface. "What on earth?"

The heat of the day had given way to a beautiful afternoon with cool eastern breezes, so London had opened one of the exterior doors to let the smell of freshly brewed coffee lure customers inside. However, her incoming customer had four paws and a wagging tail. "Friend of yours?"

"No. Never seen this one before. And no leash? Hey, you. Who'd you escape from?"

The golden retriever paused long enough to survey the surroundings and seemingly judge his welcome, spotted Rosie, and slowly padded across the floor for a sniff. Rosie eyed the much larger dog with a tilt of her chin and a few sniffs of her own before settling back down on her bed with a jingle of her bell-collar. The beautiful golden lowered himself to the floor beside the bed and Rosie, propped his chin on the cushion, and settled in as though preparing for a nap. "They certainly seem to know each other."

"How? She's never outside without me, and sadly I remember dogs and their names better than I do people." London moved across the floor and squatted down beside the golden, petting his large head. "Maybe Rosie just knows he's a good boy? Yes, you are."

Ireland laughed when London's voice went into doggy-talk mode. "Does he have a collar?"

"Such a good boy. Yes, you are. Ah, there it is. You were hiding it with all that fur, weren't you? Huh? What's your name? Ooh, Rocco. Hey, Rocco. Where did you come from? Oh, good, there's a number."

"I'm on it."

London rattled off the digits while she continued to pet Rocco, and Ireland tapped them into her cell phone and waited for the call to connect. "No answer. I'll leave a mess— Hi, I'm calling from London's Lattes to let you know your dog Rocco wandered in. We'll keep him here for you to pick up. Thanks."

"Did the message give a name?"

"No, it was one of those automated things."

London continued petting the large dog and talking in doggy-voice while Rocco simply snuffled out a sigh and relaxed even more.

"You think he's hungry?"

Ireland sipped her drink and shrugged. "Doesn't seem to be. Just tired. At least he's not pestering Rosie."

"Yeah, I know. Isn't that weird how they're just so…"

"Calm? Yeah, totally. You're sure you don't remember him?"

"Positive. But hopefully his owner will be in to get him soon." London ran her hand over the dog's head a few more times before standing and returning to the area behind the bar, where she washed her hands. "Now back to you."

"What about me?"

"Ireland, come on. When are you going to go on a date? You've been asked. I know you have."

"Yeah, mostly by men out of earshot of their wives at the inn." It was amazing what men would say despite the ring on their finger. Added to what she'd been through with her ex and the divorce and she couldn't help but think finding a good man was like searching for that proverbial needle in a haystack. "I'm busy. It's tough being a single parent."

"Which is all the more reason to date, so maybe one day you won't have to go it alone anymore."

"Who has time? And why is this all about me? You've been asked out, too, but you're just as single as I am."

"I date, though. When someone intrigues me," London added when Ireland shot her a disbelieving look. "Okay, fine, not many intrigue me enough to put forth the effort, I'll admit, but I go when it happens. My point is that you haven't gone on a single date since you moved here. Nada. I don't have the backup support you have for the inn and pier house, but… I date. What's your excuse besides fear?"

What was her excuse? Wasn't having her heart ripped out good enough? "You know I've always been… picky. Besides, I don't want to date just to have something to do on a Friday night. Dating should be about more than that."

"Agreed. But before you can get to that something 'more,' there has to be an actual get-to-know-them date first. Right?"

"I suppose. But Sammy requires all of the energy and attention I can—"

"Mooom, guess what?" Samuel ran into the coffee shop through the open door, skidding to a halt in front of Ireland. "I did it! You gotta come watch me!"

Ireland grinned at her son before shooting a purposeful glance at her sister. "See?"

"Uh, yeah. I definitely see something."

London's gaze wasn't on Ireland, though. Or Samuel. Ireland turned to see what London referred to and caught her breath as Dominic Dunn's broad shoulders filled the doorway. He stepped inside, and for the first time since he'd checked in last night, he wore a relaxed smile that highlighted his ruggedly handsome features.

And all she could do was… see.

Chapter 7

Dominic entered the coffee shop behind Samuel and smiled at the boy's enthusiasm. The kid had a great arm, and once he'd learned the mechanics, he'd improved with every throw.

"You must be Dominic."

He removed his sunglasses as he walked deeper into the building, taking the brunette's hand in his own. "London, right?"

"That's right."

"Cool! Whose dog?"

Samuel ran over to where a large golden retriever stretched out on the floor beside a wiener dog wearing a turquoise skull-and-crossbones collar. London quickly explained the situation.

"Can we keep him if his owner doesn't show up?"

"His owner *will* show up," Ireland told her son. "It's only been a few minutes since we called to let them know where he is."

"Ahhh, man," Samuel muttered, his disappointment obvious.

"Hey, what happened to how excited you were just a second ago?"

"And what kind of reaction is that when poor little Rosie is listening? You're going to hurt her feelings," London said to her nephew.

"Sorry, Rosie." Samuel stopped petting the retriever long enough to stroke the small dog's long body a few times. "But you're not a big dog like this one. I bet he'd be good at fetching a Frisbee."

"Hurtful," London said with a teasing wink at Samuel. "Good thing Rosie and I love you. You want some cold water?"

"Yes, please."

"Dominic? Would you like a drink?"

"Uh, yeah. A sweet tea sounds good, thanks."

"Coming right up."

"Do you mind if I sit?" he asked Ireland.

"No, of course not."

"We were actually just discussing you," London said, handing Ireland a kid's cup of ice water before turning back to make his drink.

Dominic would have to be blind to miss the look exchanged between the two sisters. "Oh?"

"Yes. Ireland said you were planning to leave today but stayed to help Samuel. As his unofficial favorite aunt, we appreciate that."

"It was fun. I haven't been on the ball field in a few years. I didn't realize how much I've missed it."

"There are a few pickup games around between area groups," London said. "You should join in for a game. If you decide to stay, I mean."

"Will you?" Samuel asked. "It'd be cool to see the grown-ups play."

"You've never been to a baseball game? A grown-up one?"

"No. Mom always says we'll go to a Sharks game sometime but we still haven't."

London tapped on her phone like she answered a text.

"Patience," Ireland said to her son. "We will go soon."

"Well, Wednesday is your day off," London murmured, lifting her head to smile at her sister. "And according to this," she said, waving the phone like a trophy, "there's a game that day. You guys should totally go."

"Can we? Please, Mom? Dominic, you wanna come, too?"

"Mr. Dunn," Ireland corrected.

"Actually, I hope it's okay but I told him to call me Dominic. Mr. Dunn makes me think I'm at work."

"Can we? Can he, Mom?"

"I-I suppose we could but Dominic is leaving—"

"I wouldn't mind," Dominic said, surprising himself more than Ireland with the words. "If you don't mind, that is. I don't want to intrude on your mother-son time, or your day off, but the truth of it is if I return to Atlanta too early, my coworkers won't allow me back in the office."

"Aren't you a partner? I thought I remembered Lisa telling me that?"

He lowered his head, a huff of a laugh emerging from his chest. "Yeah, I am, but Lisa arranged the trip with them, too, and I was all but thrown out for the duration with instructions to follow Lisa's orders to not return until then."

"There. It's settled then," London said.

Ireland met Dominic's gaze once more. "Are you sure? Please don't let Samuel's… enthusiasm change your plans."

No, he wasn't sure staying was the best idea. But after spending the day at the pier fishing and walking the streets of Carolina Cove to and from the ball field, he realized something deep inside of him had eased. The knot in his gut he'd had ever since that visit to the doctor's office with Lisa had loosened its grip, and he felt like he could take a deep breath for the first time in three years. Which was, no doubt, Lisa's intent when planning the surprise and enlisting his coworkers and friends, thereby ensuring his cooperation. "A few more days to honor the gift Lisa gave me by doing this, and then I can go home without anyone saying too much."

"So you're staying? Awesome! Aunt London, I'm going to a ball game!"

LATER THAT SAME EVENING, Dominic slowed the powerful Porsche near the boat launch at Fort Fisher and watched as the sun blasted the sky with the last remaining rays of the day.

After cooling off inside the coffeehouse, he and Ireland had walked to the yard beside the pavilion so Samuel could show his mom what he'd learned. Ireland was suitably impressed for a mother who obviously didn't know much about baseball, but Samuel beamed beneath the praise and approval.

Like he had been the few years he'd coached Little League, he was amazed at how much kids blossomed when given some dedicated, distraction-free moments.

Samuel needed his father, and Dominic knew there would come a day when Ireland's ex would regret missing this time with his son.

While Ireland and Samuel checked on Carolina, the youngest of the sisters, currently on duty in the inn's office, he'd gone to grab some groceries to have in his room. The suite had a small kitchenette with a coffeepot and microwave and dorm-size refrigerator/freezer, and he picked up some snacks and a few frozen burritos to keep on hand for easy access.

"Nice car!"

He searched for the person behind the voice and spotted two women loading up kayaks. One of them waved and he lifted his hand a bit awkwardly. "Thanks."

"You look strong. Care to lend us a hand?"

He seriously doubted they needed help, seeing as how they'd managed getting the kayaks off of the rack and into the water, but felt obliged to stop. "Sure." Given the time of day, the area was rapidly emptying, so he simply put the car in Park where he was and cut the engine.

"My hero," the one woman said as he approached. "I'm Beth. This is Carol."

"Nice to meet you. Dominic."

"Love the name. Are you from the area?"

Dominic eyed the bolder of the two women warily. "No. Vacationing."

He loaded the kayaks. "That should do it," he said once the second was in place. He watched Carol expertly secure them and confirm the fact the women were seasoned at doing this on their own.

Beth informed him that Carol's husband didn't like to kayak but, since Beth was single, she and Carol ventured out together. And relied on strong men such as himself to help them out when they returned tired from paddling.

He double-checked the tie-downs to make certain they'd hold once the ladies got the vehicle moving.

"Oh, you're married," Carol said.

He stepped back and nodded. "I was married twenty-one years."

"Was?" Beth asked.

Realizing he'd opened a door he couldn't go back and shut given the verbal slip, Dominic shifted his weight from foot to foot. When would saying Lisa was dead ever get easier? "I'm a widower. My wife passed away a year ago."

"Oh, how sad." Beth's comment seemed heartfelt and he accepted it as such.

"I'm sorry for your loss," Carol added. "I lost my first husband to a heart attack. He was only thirty-four. It was a hard few years, but then I met my George. We'll be married six years this September."

He nodded since he wasn't sure what the proper response was and stepped toward his car. "I, uh, should get back."

"Don't rush off," Beth said. "Hang on just a sec. Just a second."

Beth left them to quickly get something from the driver's seat. She returned and placed her hand on his forearm and slid it down the length to his fingers, where she squeezed them, pressing something into his palm.

He made eye contact and she smiled.

"Thanks again for your help. Will you be in town long?"

"A few days. I'm… not sure yet."

"Well… maybe something will entice you to stay," Beth murmured. "Have a good evening."

He got back in his car and a quick glance in his rearview mirror let him know Beth watched until he was out of sight. It was then that he opened his hand and saw Beth's name, phone number, and an invitation to dinner written on the slip of paper.

He inhaled and pressed his back against the seat as he drove. He wasn't ready for this. Dating. And it wasn't the first time it had happened. Women at work, his neighborhood, the gym. Within a matter of hours of the news spreading of Lisa's passing, women had come out of the woodwork to bring food and… offer comfort. Whatever he needed, they'd said, the look in their eyes making it clear it could mean as little or as much as he wanted.

Some men might find it flattering and be tempted by the offers, but he wasn't one of them. His marriage had meant more to him than that. More than jumping into bed with someone else just because he was now free to do so.

Dominic drove back to Carolina Cove and into the inn's parking lot, his good mood soured by the exchange and what the future held. Maybe he was a romantic, but he'd hoped to grow old with his wife. Instead he was alone and lonelier than he ever remembered feeling.

He'd rounded the car to retrieve the groceries from the passenger side when he heard Ireland call his name.

"You dropped something," Ireland said.

He turned in time to see her stooping down to pick whatever it was up from where the breeze had blown it. She'd turned to face him, but as she closed the distance between them, he saw her glance down. He recognized the slip and knew the moment Ireland read Beth's number and message.

"Here. You, uh, wouldn't want to lose that."

"Ireland—"

"Enjoy your night."

"I didn't ask for her number."

"It's none of my business, Dominic."

"Beth— She gave it to me but I didn't ask for it."

"Again, none of my business."

He gripped the bags so tightly that his fingers hurt. "Are we still on for the game this week?"

"Um, yeah. I guess. I'm taking Sammy for sure, but if your plans don't change and you're still here, you're welcome to join us."

"Thanks. I'd like that." He'd sensed her reluctance before, but now he got the impression she was even more hesitant. He could see it in her expression.

"Okay then. Night."

She'd taken a step or two away from him when he said, "Samuel keeps asking for a ride in my car. I thought maybe I'd drive to the game. If you wouldn't mind, that is. He might get a kick out of it."

Once again he noted the differences in Ireland and Beth. Beth had been drawn to the Porsche but Ireland glanced at the car, her expression lacking enthusiasm.

"I suppose we could. Sammy does really want to ride in it, and to be honest, I hate driving in traffic."

"Sounds like a plan. Wait, would you like me to walk you home? It's getting dark."

Ireland lifted her hand and pushed at the hair blowing into her face in the breeze.

"I'm good. Enjoy your… evening."

Chapter 8

The next morning, Ireland stopped by London's Lattes on the way to the inn. Samuel remained two steps ahead of her and drew her attention to the fact Rocco was still there. "His owner didn't show up?"

London glanced up from what she was doing and shook her head. "Didn't have to. After you left last night, I had a wave of people, and he snuck out when I wasn't looking. The owner didn't call, though, so I'm guessing Rocco made it home."

"But now he's back."

"Yup. Showed up about ten minutes ago and lay down by Rosie, same as yesterday."

Samuel dropped to his knees beside the dogs and was greeted with licks and wagging tails.

"Are you going to call the owner again?" Ireland asked as she leaned against the bar.

"Not as long as he behaves himself. He's got to be local. Maybe a new family moved in and they aren't aware of the leash laws. I just hope Rocco doesn't get reported and picked up."

Ireland watched as Samuel told Rocco to sit and the dog immediately complied, tail sweeping the floor. He proceeded to shake, lie down, and roll over.

"So are you and Sammy excited about going to the game?"

Ireland narrowed her gaze on her younger sister and wished she could muster up more enthusiasm. "I guess." She lowered her voice. "You know you didn't have to go Googling the schedule like you did."

"Oh, come on. It's a few hours of fun with a handsome man and your son. Besides, it's supposed to be cooler on Wednesday, so at least you won't be baking in those seats."

"And we get to ride in Dominic's cool car!" Samuel said from the floor.

"Oh, really. He's driving… a cool car?"

Ireland rolled her eyes. "Yes, he's driving. I ran into him last night at the inn, and he offered to drive since Sammy wants a ride and it would be odd to hand my kid off to a man I barely know."

"Agreed. And the cool car is…?"

"A brand-new Porsche."

"Wowza. Nice."

"Eh."

London propped her elbows on the countertop and laced her fingers together. "I know you love your car, but you are our father's daughter, and you went to every one of those car shows with us. You like fast cars just as much as we all do."

"Okay, fine. Yes, it's a nice car, but I don't get spending that kind of money on something like that. It probably cost as much as a house."

"Is that the reason? Or because it makes you think of your ex?"

Ireland glared at London before checking to see if Samuel still listened. Thankfully her son had taken to playing with the dogs on the far side of the room and was currently reading the dogs a book from the kids' section. "Do you mind not saying stuff like that in front of him?"

"Sammy isn't listening now, and you know I checked before I said it. What's up with you? Answer the question."

"Nothing is up. And Rich had to have the best of the best whether we could afford it or not. He'd just roll the difference into the new vehicle and pretend we weren't in debt."

"Okay. What's that got to do with Dominic?"

"Nothing. It has nothing to do with Dominic. You're right. I don't know anything about his or Lisa's finances, and I shouldn't be judging someone for driving a car costing more than I make in a year."

"But you are."

"It doesn't seem a bit… suspect to you? A handsome widower, a flashy car. He's in mourning, I know it because I see it and Lisa warned me he would be. I just wonder if he's trying to comfort himself in… questionable ways."

"Questionable ways?" London straightened. "Okay, now I know something's up. Explain."

Ireland lifted her hands in the air as though surrendering. "It's *nothing*. I need to just shut up and stop overthinking everything."

"Uh-uh. You're not getting out of it that easily. What do you mean by 'questionable ways'?"

Ireland pulled at one of her earrings and sighed. "When I left the office last night, Dominic was getting out of the car," she said dryly. "He dropped something and I picked it up. I didn't mean to look but it was a woman's name, number, and a message to call her for dinner." When London stared at her blankly, Ireland huffed. "He went to the grocery store, for pity's sake. He wasn't gone for more than an hour, tops."

London stepped back from the bar and… grinned. *"What?"*

"You. You act like you're—dare I say it?—jealous."

"How can I be jealous? I only just met the man."

"I have no idea how you can be jealous, but you're definitely acting like it."

"I'm not. I'm… indignant. On Lisa's behalf. She arranged this trip for him—"

"A year after her death," London interjected. "Maybe this is exactly what Lisa had in mind."

"Picking up a random woman while on a grocery run? I seriously doubt that."

"No, really. I've been thinking about this ever since we talked yesterday— you know, my point about it being her last goodbye? If you were her, wouldn't you think him meeting someone was a distinct possibility? The man is quite handsome."

Ireland frowned down at her chipped fingernail polish before glancing at her watch. She needed to get her caffeine fix before taking over for the night manager. "I don't know. Maybe. Is my coffee ready?"

"Stop changing the subject."

"I don't like talking to you about this."

London laughed. "Only because you know I might

be right. Ireland, you're looking at it from the view of a loving wife—"

"Well, of course I am."

"—who is still *here*. That's why you're upset. As a *wife*, you know what it did to you when Rich flirted with other women right in front of you."

"I hated it. I told him over and over again, but he didn't care that it hurt me."

"Exactly. But what if you looked at it from the view of a *dead* wife who's loving her husband from beyond? She did love him, right?"

"Yes." That much she knew for certain. Lisa had been teary while making the arrangements, but she'd also been… accepting. Not in the sense of her impending death but… excited to be doing something for Dominic to surprise him, help him.

"So what if she *hoped* he'd come here and enjoy himself and maybe remember what it's like to be single? He's still young, handsome—"

"So you've mentioned more than once."

"Because it's true. Look, you haven't let go of the hurt Rich caused you, and I get it. I do. But Dominic can't betray someone who's no longer here."

As much as she hated to admit it, London was right. "I didn't think of it that way."

London blew on her fingertips and rubbed them against her shirt while making an I-told-you-so face.

"It doesn't mean you're right," Ireland added. "Just that I hadn't thought of it that way."

"So did he go to dinner?"

She pressed her fingertips to her temple and sighed. "Am I ever going to get my coffee?"

Chapter 9

Midmorning the following day, Dominic was sitting on one of the benches on the pier watching the waves roll in, a fresh cup of coffee from London's Lattes in his hand.

There had been a few people there with laptops working and a mug in front of them, and Rocco the golden retriever was back too, showing up just as Dominic had turned to leave. The dog had tail-wagged his way over to Rosie's bed and plopped down, same as before.

Screeching from below drew his attention, and Dominic spotted someone jumping up and waving their arms, a flock of sea birds scattering at the commotion but not going very far.

A lifeguard blew his whistle and motioned, indicating that someone was swimming too close to the pier.

Dominic took a sip and went back to people watching, squinting behind his sunglasses when he spotted a kid Samuel's size and appearance walking toward the pier with a couple of other, bigger boys. The Samuel look-alike held a bag of some kind.

Samuel walked slowly, keeping an eye on the boys as they ran toward the dunes. "What are you up to?" Dominic murmured under his breath.

Sure enough, Samuel stopped and opened the bag he held and tossed a chip toward a nearby bird, which alerted every bird in a mile radius to come join the party. Birds flocked, squawked, and everyone in the general vicinity watched as Samuel tossed chips into the air. Beachgoers left their beach towels and chairs with cell phones in hand to snap photos of the many, many birds—and while all of that was happening, the two kids who'd moved toward the dunes quickly peeked into unattended coolers left behind by Samuel's audience and snagged drinks from within. "You little thieves."

Dominic watched as the boys walked toward the pier. Samuel noted his buddies leaving him and ended the show. He wadded up the top of the bag to close it and started running to catch up.

Dominic watched the other boys and noted the stolen drinks. The shorter of the two carried what looked to be water and a sports drink given the color, but the oldest of the trio tucked his beneath his shirt to carry.

They quickly disappeared beneath the pier, and Dominic lost sight of them thanks to the summer crowd and distance.

He shook his head, wondering what Samuel's dad was thinking abandoning not only his wife but his child in a world where, every day, they faced a battle of some kind.

. . .

"WHERE HAVE YOU BEEN? I've been calling everywhere looking for you," Ireland said to Samuel the moment he walked into the inn's office just before lunch.

"Around. We went to the beach."

"We?"

"Some boys from school."

"What boys?"

"Just a couple of guys from the older league."

"And you behaved yourself?"

"Yes, ma'am."

Ireland jerked a thumb toward the break room behind the counter. "Carolina brought lunch on her way in. You must be hungry by now."

"No thanks."

"No?" She stopped restocking the snack box and made eye contact with Samuel. "What'd you eat? You're always starving by noon."

"We had some stuff."

"What stuff, where'd you get it, and who paid for it?"

The door behind Samuel chimed, and she looked up to find Dominic slipping inside. "Dominic, what can I help you with today?"

"Actually, I saw Samuel and thought I'd ask your permission to go fishing on the pier again."

"Yes! For real?"

"For real. But only if your mom says it's okay." He met Ireland's gaze and paused. Had her eyes always been that color? Maybe it was the turquoise blouse she wore that made them seem brighter than he remembered, but her eyes drew him... "Sorry if I'm interrupting."

"No, not at all. And I suppose it's okay if he goes.

Samuel's been missing in action all morning, but he swears he's behaved himself. Right, Samuel?"

Dominic looked at Samuel and saw the kid staring at the floor. Uh-huh.

He'd seen the boys' latest antics when the remaining potato chips were getting thrown *off* the pier so that the birds swarmed unsuspecting tourists. This fishing opportunity wasn't about a reward so much as keeping an eye on the kid while curbing his own boredom as a man used to working every day. "Go grab your gear. Don't forget a pole for me. Bait is my treat."

Samuel took off toward the back of the building.

"You don't have to do this."

"I know I don't. But lying on the beach isn't my thing, and I like to fish. If Samuel wears out and wants to do something else, I'll make sure I return him here first for permission."

"Oh, hello. Who are you?"

A woman emerged from the rear of the office area, and Dominic knew he stared at yet another of the sisters.

"Carolina, this is Dominic Dunn. He's in the third-floor suite."

"Oh, yeah, I heard— Nice to meet you."

"Likewise." Carolina looked very much like her sister, but her bohemian style and flowy clothing left her appearing more flower child than beachgoer. "Oh, Ireland, I just ran some local kids out of the pool. Gonna have to keep an eye out."

"It's that time of year," Ireland said, rolling her eyes. "Doesn't help that they know Dad is out of town. They're more afraid of him than they are of us."

Dominic smiled at the image. Ex-military soldier

versus two women who'd probably order them out but check them for signs of tears and offer a snack before they left the area? Yeah, he'd bet on the kids. "Local tradition?"

The ladies glanced at each other, and Ireland raised a telling eyebrow.

Carolina grinned. "You could say that."

Ireland huffed out a sound that was part laugh, part groan. "Maybe for you. As the eldest, I was the one who was always responsible when you wouldn't mind orders and went pool hopping." She shook her head at Dominic. "The local motels and HOAs had *fits*."

"Well, if Dad would've allowed us to swim in our pool, we wouldn't have had to go elsewhere."

"The pool is for paying guests. Like I tell Samuel, he gets to swim in off-season and slow times. Especially when the rules are kids have to be accompanied by adults and I can't be out there when I'm working in here."

"Ahhh. That was the trick," Carolina informed them, nodding. "Tagging just the right adult so that it looked like we were with them or with their kids so we didn't get caught."

He chuckled at the antics. "So you didn't go pool hopping with her?" he asked Ireland.

"I'm eight years older so no. When she was doing all of that, I was working or going to school."

"Yeah. The problem with being the youngest in the family is that I missed out on all the real fun. They got to travel the world as kids whenever our dad was reassigned overseas while I've been stuck here most of my life."

"Ready!"

"Sunscreen?" Ireland asked her son.

"Ah, man." Samuel released a heavy-laden sigh and dumped the load he carried onto the floor at his feet before racing back down the hallway behind the desk.

"Don't worry about bait. I'll make a call to the pier house and tell them Samuel is coming to fish so they can help keep an eye on him."

"It's no problem."

Maybe it was what Lisa had claimed to be mother's intuition, but Dominic knew Ireland had picked up on something when her gaze narrowed on him.

"Is there something you're not telling me?"

He moved into the room enough to snag the poles and tackle box.

"Dominic…?"

Knowing he'd want to know if it was his child—and having already been through the underage-drinking stage with his own kids—he paused. "I saw some behavior today that needs addressing… before it potentially becomes a problem later. Look," he said, glancing down the hallway to where Samuel had disappeared. "I've raised two kids and coached ornery Little League boys for several years. It's nothing I haven't had to handle before in one way or another. I'll talk to him. Okay?"

Her shoulders slumped. "Dominic, just tell me. What was it? Sneaking smelly bait in coolers? Changing the words on portable signs? Pool hopping like the kids Carolina just ran off?"

He whistled. "Dang, the kids here are busy in summer."

"You have *no* idea. Now what has my little darling been up to?"

Carolina giggled. "From that expression, I'm guessing more than one of the above."

"Really?"

Ireland looked horrified as only a concerned mother could.

Samuel raced back into the room, a huge grin on his face and a smear of white down his nose. "Ready."

"You know, I'm craving some chips. You don't have a bag to bring with us, do you?" he said to the boy.

Ireland's eyes widened slightly before narrowing on her son. "Sure we do. We have a brand-new bag in the cabinet," she said. "Sammy, go get it."

Samuel's face paled to the shade of the sunscreen on his nose and his eyes got as big as saucers. "Uh… It's gone. I got hungry."

"You ate an entire bag of chips?"

"I shared some."

"With whom?"

"Um… just the kids from school."

"What kids?"

Obviously not wanting to rat out his friends, Samuel lifted a bony shoulder in a shrug.

"Just kids from practice. Sorry, Mom. Are you ready?" Samuel asked Dominic.

Dominic winked at Ireland. "Yup. Let's get fishing."

"HE'S HOT," Carolina said after the door had shut behind Dominic and Samuel.

"He's too old for you—and in mourning."

"Might be too old for me but he's not too old for you."

"Did you miss the *and in mourning* part?"

"Can't mourn forever. And I saw the way he was looking at you. And that wink? *Totally hot.*"

"The wink was because we were putting the screws to Samuel, and Dominic's look was one of pity because I'm doing a horrible job as a parent."

"Oh, stop it. You are not."

"Yeah? I wonder how many poor tourists got the fright of their life today thinking they were suddenly in *The Birds.* It's a wonder someone didn't call the police."

"Come on, you can't be *that* mad. It's funny and you know it."

It was. She'd seen local kids pull the stunt several times since she'd moved here, but the trickster had never been her son. "What's next? Tipping lifeguard stands?"

"That's better than cows. At least no animals are hurt during the tipping."

Once more Carolina grinned, and Ireland shoved her fingers into her hair as though to pull it out, unable to stop the smile that formed. "He's being a normal boy, right? Do you think this is because of his dad?"

"Sammy's doing great, all things considered."

"Maybe. But he's only ten. What's he going to be doing at twelve? Thirteen?" She gulped. "*Sixteen?*"

"Hmm… That's a tough one. But based on what I did with my friends at that age and if you refuse to date, you'd better hope this is Dad's last vacation until Sammy turns twenty-one. Just saying."

Chapter 10

"So, you going to open that bag of chips we got?" Dominic was watching Samuel when he posed the question and saw the boy's guilty expression.

"You saw, didn't you?"

"Yup."

"We were just having fun."

"You stole drinks from people."

"I didn't."

"You were part of the crew, Samuel. That makes you just as guilty as the boys who took those drinks from the coolers while you distracted the people. What were they, anyway?"

Samuel scuffed his shoes along the lower rung of the pier railing and shrugged. "I got water."

"And the others?" Dominic cast his line and waited.

"A Gatorade and… one of 'em was a beer. But I didn't drink any. Jon— Just the other boys did."

"I see."

"I promise I didn't drink any. Are you going to tell my mom?"

"Don't you think I should?"

"She won't let me go to the game tomorrow if you do."

"If stealing is something you plan to do all summer, maybe you shouldn't be allowed to go."

Samuel lowered his chin to his chest. "I'm sorry. I didn't know they were going to steal. Honest. We were just messing around with the chips and laughing at the tourists freaking out. They bet me I couldn't throw some in the air and get fifty people to watch."

It sounded like Samuel had been suckered into participating by the older boys, but it didn't change the end result. "Yeah, well, here's the thing—you are who you hang out with, and by association, whether you knew it or not, today you stole something that wasn't yours."

"Really?"

"Really. So before you run around with boys who steal for fun, you need to ask yourself if that's who you want to be. It might seem like pranks now, but if you're hanging with those kids and they do something more serious, the police will be involved. They could have been called today had you been caught, and you'd be just as guilty as those other boys because you were with them. That's something you need to think about."

"Yeah. I guess."

Dominic felt a tug on his line and patiently waited. Once his line tightened, he did a little tugging of his own.

"You've got one!"

He began reeling and peered over the railing to see the flash of silver in the water below. "Not very big."

"Bring him up! Let's see!"

He laughed at Samuel's enthusiasm for what looked like the smallest fish ever and was surprised to find a baby shark on the other end of his hook. People passing by paused to see what he'd caught and take a look as Dominic unhooked it and dropped it down into the water below.

He settled himself back onto the bench beside Samuel, who had reeled in his line and was attaching a different kind of bait.

"Are you going to tell my mom about stealing the drinks and the… beer?"

"No." Dominic glanced at Samuel and held the boy's gaze. "You're going to tell her."

"But… she's gonna be really sad. And mad. I don't want to make her cry."

"Then I guess that's something else to consider before you pull a stunt like that again, isn't it? How your mom and grandparents and family will feel."

Samuel's chin trembled and the kid swallowed hard.

"Look, Sam, I'm guessing your mom will be happy you told her. Honesty is important, and so long as you've learned your lesson and you don't do it again—"

"I won't. I really won't. Grandpa'd be so mad at me. But I didn't know they'd done it until I got under the pier and saw them." His head lowered and the boy's mouth twisted down. "I guess I should've known they didn't really want to hang out with me. Mason kinda laughed when Christopher asked me." Samuel cast again and plopped down onto the bench.

"So they're older boys?"

Samuel shrugged. "Yeah. I think Christopher's fourteen."

"You don't have buddies your age you can hang out with?"

"Yeah, but a lot of 'em are on vacation or… doing stuff with their dads."

"You miss your dad, huh?"

The boy shrugged again but Dominic could read the truth in Samuel's expression. "Well, I don't know how long your grandpa will be gone, but maybe we can hang out some while I'm here. If your mom agrees to it— *after* you tell her about the stunt earlier."

"Do I really have to tell her?"

"Men have to accept responsibility for their actions, good and bad."

"Maaan. I hope she doesn't cancel the game."

Dominic reached over and ruffled the kid's hair. "Me, too, buddy. Me, too."

Chapter 11

Dominic found himself back on the pier near sunset, facing the wind and watching as the last of the sun's rays lit up the sky in bright reds and oranges.

He and Samuel had fished for a couple of hours then grabbed some burgers for dinner before Samuel headed off to baseball practice. The kid had promised to talk to his mom and confess, and Dominic wondered what Ireland's decision would be regarding the ball game tomorrow. On the one hand, he could see the need for punishment, but on the other hand, he also saw Samuel's need for such time, to refill the well neglected by his missing father.

"Dominic! Hello there."

Dominic turned and found Carol, one of the kayaking ladies, standing nearby, on the opposite side of the chain-link fence closing the pier to general access. Everyone had to enter or exit through the pier house during the season.

"I thought that was you standing there. Beautiful sunset, isn't it?"

He nodded his agreement and took in the bike she was locking up for safekeeping.

"Hang on and I'll join you. If you don't mind, that is? I walk to the T every evening before I head home."

"Sure." Dominic lost sight of Carol while she made her way through the pier house, but once through the door, she approached him with a big smile. She was a pretty woman for her age, which he guessed to be close to sixty.

"So have you decided to stay for a few days or are you out here saying goodbye?"

"I'm going to stay on a few days."

"I'd be surprised if you didn't. Rarely is anyone ever in a hurry to leave. I love living here. Maybe while you're here you'll run into someone who can show you the highlights."

"Uh… Maybe." He wasn't sure what else to say since he was pretty sure Carol meant her friend Beth.

His thoughts must have shown on his face because Carol laughed softly. "Don't worry. I won't tell Beth I ran into you or she'll be hanging out here hoping to see you again."

"Thanks."

"You haven't dated anyone since your wife passed, have you?"

He was surprised by Carol's forthrightness but the expression she wore was one of sympathy. Dominic tossed his empty coffee cup into a trash can and shoved his hands into his pockets. "Is it that obvious?"

"A little. But only because I recognize the look of dread since I wore it for so long."

He glanced down at the woman and realized they

shared more than some might think. "My last first date was twenty-four years ago. That doesn't seem… real."

She chuckled and nodded. "That just confirms you're a good man, Dominic. I've known other widowers. Their wives were barely in the grave and they were out looking. It was sad and disrespectful, in my opinion. Like the person was as replaceable as a light bulb."

"That's not love," he said in agreement.

"No, it isn't. But your wife… You said she's been gone a year. Am I remembering that right?" Carol frowned and shaded her eyes with her hand. "Look. Dolphins."

He followed to where she pointed, and three fins broke surface nearly at the same time. "That's right, a year. Do you see dolphins often?"

"Almost daily. Just have to watch for them."

He inhaled and, because his gut told him Carol would indeed understand, quickly filled her in as to Lisa's preplanned trip for him.

"That's… that's just so thoughtful." Carol wiped away tears from behind her sunglasses. "What a gift to receive. She obviously loved you as much as you loved her."

"I think so, too."

"Well, I'm so glad you decided to stay a few more days at least. May I ask what changed your mind?"

"A couple of things, I guess. I don't want to be disrespectful of the effort she put into planning this whole thing and… I found myself making plans."

"Plans. As in…?" Carol's expression changed from surprise to pleasure. "A date?"

"No, no. Not like that." He leaned his forearms against the railing and scanned the surface for more dolphins. "It just kind of came about. There's this kid, a local. I helped him with a baseball pitch, and he mentioned he's never been to a game."

"His parents are allowing him to go with a stranger?"

"No. Technically, his mother is taking him. I'm the one tagging along because the kid asked me to join them."

"A single mother?"

"Yeah. But it's not a date," he quickly said.

"Is she pretty?"

The question gave him pause. "She's... beautiful."

"Nice?"

"Very."

"So why not make it a practice date then?"

"A practice date?"

"Well, does the mother think she's going on a date?"

"No. It's for her son. An experience for him. If we wind up going. He got into some trouble today," he explained. "So she may cancel."

"Would you be disappointed if she did?"

Once again Dominic was taken aback by Carol's questions, but after a long moment, he nodded. "Yeah. I think I would be. I haven't done anything like that in years."

"Hmm. Well, all the more reason to have a practice date if you do go. She'll be none the wiser. If you go, go, have fun. Practice your flirting *if* you feel like it, and just enjoy the day without the pressure of a real date. Then when you're ready and decide to go on a real date, it won't be as stressful."

"Is that what you did? Is this experience talking?" He straightened from his slouched position and turned toward her, watching as her smile lit her face with happiness.

"How did you guess? My George was sneaky. He knew I was afraid of falling in love again after being so broken by my husband's passing, so instead of asking me on a date, he'd just show up and it would turn into one. This is a small town when all of the tourists are gone. It was easy to find ourselves at the same place, and George… He'd ask me to dance or bring me a drink. Sit beside me. We met at different events for months before we went on an official date, and I didn't realize until afterward that he'd planned it all along."

"That is sneaky."

"George said he knew he had to creep into my heart before I shut him out of it because of fear. And all I can say is that I'm glad he did."

Carol placed her hand on his arm, but instead of the contact feeling overtly sexual like had with Beth, with Carol it felt friendly and comforting.

"Speaking of which, I should head home to my George. He's ready for dinner by now. Enjoy your time here, Dominic, especially the ball game. Life is short, as we both know. Take a chance and live while you can."

Chapter 12

Dominic walked Carol through the pier house and out onto the boardwalk, where she retrieved her bike and headed home.

A short time later, he sat at the bar of Eddie's Restaurant pondering the menu when Ireland came through the door. He watched as she chatted briefly with the hostess before heading his way. He knew the moment she spotted him due to the hesitation in her step. "Evening."

"Good evening," Ireland said. "I'm glad I ran into you. Can we talk?"

"Sure. Why don't you join me?"

He could practically see her going over the pros and cons in her mind, but a moment later, she took the stool beside him.

"Would you like a drink?" the bartender asked.

"Uh, yeah, thank you," she murmured. "A sweet tea, please." She flashed a smile in his direction. "After my talk with Samuel, I'd like something stronger than tea but feel the need to keep a clear head."

"Ahh, he told you about the beer."

"Oh, yeah. Sammy told me all about the boys stealing the drinks and the chip fiasco with the tourists as well as a few other things I didn't really want to know. Once he got started, I think he felt the need for a cleansing and decided to tell every deep, dark secret he held."

Dominic chuckled at the image, well able to imagine Samuel doing just that in the hopes of redeeming himself. "He's a good kid."

"I know he is. A handful at the moment, but good."

"For what it's worth, I think he's telling the truth about not knowing what the older ones had planned. I could see them duping him given the age difference."

"They're lucky they weren't caught and taken to task by the owners right there on the beach, much less caught drinking the beer." She met his gaze. "He said he didn't drink it, and maybe I'd prefer to keep the blinders on, but I believe him. But even if he didn't do it today, what if there's a next time?"

"Cross that bridge when you come to it. Maybe there won't be a next time."

"Well, I appreciate what you said to him, about becoming who his friends are and being careful who he chooses. I think it resonated with him."

"I'm glad. It's something my father shared with me at that age and something I shared with my son and the kids on the ball teams I coached."

The bartender set Ireland's drink in front of her.

"Here's to surviving parenthood," he said, lifting his glass.

She lifted her iced tea and lightly clinked it with his.

"Sammy also told me what you said about hanging out with you while you're here."

"Speaking of which, what did you decide about the game tomorrow? Are we still on?"

Ireland twisted her mouth in a wry grimace. "I'm not sure." She shot him an inquisitive glance. "I don't suppose you have any insight about that, seeing as how you've already raised a son?"

"I've thought about that all day, actually."

"And?"

"I'd take him. It's a time to bond and praise his honesty and remorse. Hopefully it will instill more confidence in being a good person and behaving himself, and that'll keep him from the wrong sorts of friends in the future. At least give him pause when it comes into play."

She nodded slowly and inhaled. "After he spilled his guts and came clean, I hated the thought of not taking him."

"Sounds like we're on the same page then."

"But what you said… You do remember you're on vacation, right? You should be going out, touring Southport and Wilmington, doing fun things. Not babysitting my son."

"Hey, cut me some slack. It's my first vacation in years, so I'm out of practice. Besides, Samuel is proving to be quite entertaining."

She laughed and shook her head, and he liked the way the smile transformed her from worried mom to beautiful woman.

He shifted uncomfortably on the stool because of the thought. It felt disrespectful to Lisa but… it didn't change the fact it was true or that it wasn't the first time he'd noticed Ireland's beauty.

"He is that."

Brought back to the topic at hand, he asked, "What about you?"

"What about me?"

"When do you get to go on vacation?"

Her long lashes lowered over her eyes. "Ahh, hmm… It's different when you live and work at the beach."

"What, you don't vacation? Or does that require a trip to the mountains away from your guests and everyone needing your attention? Have you actually done all of the stuff you just mentioned since you moved here?"

"I thought we were talking about you?"

He sipped his drink but lifted a finger from the glass and pointed it in her direction. "That's a no."

"I've been… busy."

"Are you ready to order?" the bartender asked them.

Carol's words about practice dating came to mind, and while he wasn't sure he was even ready for a practice date, they both had to eat. "Join me for dinner. I've eaten every meal alone since I arrived, so the least you can do is keep me company."

"That's not true. We ate together on the pier." She shifted on the stool and shoved the menu toward the bartender without looking at it. "But I will," she added with a nod. "Just give me the pasta special and one to go, please."

"I'll take the same. And add her order to my bill."

"Oh, no. Dominic, I can't accept."

"I insist," he said, nodding toward the bartender, who stepped back to go put in the order.

"Thank you but you don't have to do that. I should be buying you dinner for your talk with Samuel."

"Like I said. Entertainment. That kid has made me laugh more in the last couple of days than I have in the last year. It's fine. Besides, Lisa spoke of you often. She really enjoyed her time here and thought of you and your family as friends. I'm grateful for the time you spent with her and how you welcomed her."

"Her girls' weekend with her friend was a pleasure to see. Lisa seemed like a wonderful woman."

"She was."

"My situation is different, as you know, but I imagine that sense of loneliness is about the same."

He nodded. "It's not easy starting over, is it? A friend of mine went through a bad divorce about the same time as Lisa's passing. I think he had a harder time accepting the end of his marriage than I did Lisa's death." He felt her staring at him as though in surprise. "Did I sound insensitive?"

"No, it's just… I've tried to explain that to my family but they don't get it. It's horrible regardless of how a marriage ends, but it's *different* when someone you love chooses to walk away."

"My buddy says the same thing."

Ireland fiddled with the paper napkin beneath her glass, a multitude of expressions flickering across her features in a matter of seconds. Dominic watched, fascinated by the play of emotions.

"My family insists that I need to start dating. I don't know about you, but who wants to put themselves out there again after what we've been through? It takes guts and I'm not sure I'm that brave. Not anymore."

Dominic stared at her, drawn by her words, her expression. He felt the same way. Which made him wonder what it was about her that made him want to find his courage again.

Chapter 13

Ireland stepped from the restaurant and stared up at the darkened sky, surprised that she'd just spent the last two hours talking to Dominic. And not just talking but *conversing*. They'd discussed everything. Life, love, dating, their children, current events, favorite things to do. And a part of her was amazed at how much she'd enjoyed herself.

While she'd been sitting there eating her dinner, Frankie had texted to say practice had ended and Samuel had fallen asleep on her couch, worn out from his adventures. Her sister had ordered Ireland to enjoy a night off and get some sleep before tomorrow's game… and she hoped the guy they were going with was as good as Samuel made him out to be.

Ireland inhaled the salt air and the way the breeze carried the freshness of rain with it, knowing no matter where life took her she would always relish the scent.

"Wow. You can see the storm over the water out there."

She glanced up at Dominic's profile and then out to

sea. A thunderstorm flashed in the distance, the clouds lighting up with each glorious display. "Hmm. I love watching the thunderheads roll over the water."

"Wanna get some ice cream from the pier house and sit on the swings?"

"I couldn't eat another bite, but some time on the swings sounds nice."

They moved down the street in unison, the noise from the arcade drowning out the sound of the waves for just a moment until they moved past it and crossed the narrow street to the boardwalk.

An older gentleman was leaving the first swing across from the pavilion just as they walked by.

"Hey, Miss Ireland. Here you go. Take my spot. It's time for me to get myself home. You two enjoy yourselves."

"Thank you, Roland," Ireland murmured. "Don't drive too fast on that cart."

"I'll keep it under sixty," the man joked. "You treat her nice now," Roland said, wagging a finger at Dominic. "This pretty girl deserves a good man."

"Uh, yes, sir. I couldn't agree more."

Ireland flushed and couldn't decide if it was out of embarrassment or because of the possibility Dominic might mean what he said and find her as attractive as she did him.

So you think Lisa's husband is handsome?

But she wasn't sure what to think of that realization, only that it was true. During their time in the restaurant, Dominic had laughed and relaxed, and she'd seen a different man than the one she knew only as Lisa's husband. This man was an attractive, intelligent, funny, and seemingly genuine man.

Ireland shook her head at herself and settled on the swing, leaving plenty of room for Dominic to join her. He sat down beside her, and the breeze carried his cologne to her nose. It smelled rich and spicy, with hints of sandalwood.

She lifted her hand and brushed the hair from her face, and Dominic set the swing in motion. Unlike their nonstop conversation in the restaurant, they remained quiet, but it was a comfortable quiet.

As the lightning flashed high in the clouds out at sea, she stared in awestruck wonder at the power and beauty of it. The temperature had dropped radically from earlier in the day, the rain-cooled breeze having a chill, but the heat and size of Dominic's body beside hers kept the wind from blasting her too much.

Tourists came and went along the boardwalk, the air filled with laughter and conversation, flip-flops flapping against the planks behind them. Birds squawked as they battled the wind, and the pier lights revealed the shadows of fishermen lined up along the railings.

"I'm starting to get it," Dominic said. "Why Lisa loved it here."

The mention of his wife reminded Ireland yet again that he was a man mourning the love of his life. She crossed her arms over her front and stared off into the distance.

Dominic was the last person she needed to be thinking of as handsome or funny, especially when his plans were as unpredictable as the storm they watched.

"Are you cold? Should we go?"

Using the excuse, she nodded. "Yeah. Sorry. I need to get home."

"I'll walk you."

"It's not far. I'll be fine."

"It's not a problem. I'll need to know where to pick you and Samuel up tomorrow for the game."

Walking the four blocks to her home took longer than usual due to the congestion of summer traffic and pedestrians around the pier and pavilion, but once they crossed the intersection, things quieted and slowed, and it was more like it was in the off-season.

Every now and again, her hand or shoulder brushed Dominic's as they walked, and with every touch, her heart picked up speed. "Nice house."

"Thanks. It's Holland's," she said, leading the way up the stairs. "She works out of town so often that when Sammy and I moved here, she asked us to stay so that the house wasn't sitting empty."

When they arrived at the top and entered the screened-in porch, she noticed he paused to take in the view of the neighborhood. The house was several blocks from the water, so there wasn't an ocean view unless they continued up the stairs to the crow's nest.

She fished her key from her small purse, juggling the bag of food she'd ordered for Samuel thinking he'd be there after practice.

"Here. Allow me."

Dominic took the key and unlocked the door for her before handing it back to her. "Thanks. For dinner and walking me home."

"My pleasure."

Maybe it was the storm and the electrically charged air affecting her senses. Maybe it was the conversation they'd had in the restaurant. It could be the way Dominic spoke of his late wife with such reverence and love, but whatever it was in that moment... she felt pulled to him in a way she'd wondered if she could ever be drawn to a man again.

But why did it have to be him? Dominic, who still reeled from Lisa's death? Who lived much too far away to make dating a viable option even if he was ready?

"I should go before the storm gets here."

She quickly nodded. "Yeah, you'd better. You don't want to be struck by lightning." She held up the bagged food. "Thanks again."

"My pleasure. Good night, Ireland."

Ireland waited and watched as he left, all the while reminding herself that very soon he'd return to Atlanta, to the life he'd built with the woman he'd never get over losing.

Chapter 14

By midafternoon the game was over and they were on the way back to the island.

"That was so much fun! Can we go again sometime?"

"It was fun, and we'll see," Ireland said, flashing a smile over her shoulder to where Samuel sat in the back-seat. "What do you have to say to Dominic for driving us in his 'cool car'?"

"Thanks, Dominic! This is awesome!"

"You're welcome. Thank you for letting me tag along. That was a great game." The windows were down, and it was a gorgeous day thanks to the storms last night that had lowered the humidity and cooled the temps a bit.

Dominic glanced across the expanse of the vehicle to where Ireland sat looking every bit as adorable as her son. She wore a Sharks T-shirt and cutoff shorts that highlighted her tan legs, and he'd be lying if he said he hadn't noticed how long they were more than once.

The wind blew the curls around her face, and with

the sunglasses perched on her nose and lips rosy from the red Icee she and Samuel had shared, he found himself struggling to pay attention to the road in front of him.

"Can we ride the ferry?"

Dominic glanced in the rearview mirror and met Samuel's gaze. "To Southport?"

"Yeah! Please, Dominic? It's fun."

"Samuel, Dominic may have made plans for the day, and besides, we just went to the game."

"I know. But we're having a fun day, right? So can't we have more fun?"

Dominic laughed at the boy's statement and shared a glance with Ireland. "You can't fault his reasoning. Sound fun to you?"

"Really?"

"Why not?"

It took some time to get through the traffic, but once they crossed the bridge to the island and turned onto Dow, the ride got a little faster. In a matter of minutes, he turned onto the road taking them to the ferry, and they managed to make it onto the one currently loading. "That was some good timing, Samuel," he said, getting out of the car and holding the door for Sam to climb out.

"Let's go up on the top deck. Okay, Mom?"

"Yes, see you there in a second."

Samuel ran toward the stairs leading to the upper deck of the ferry, but Dominic waited for Ireland to gather her purse and exit the Porsche.

"Nice car," a man said as he followed his family toward the stairs. "You must have hit the lottery."

Ireland glanced up at him, and Dominic shrugged,

embarrassed by the man's comment given the attention it drew from other passengers. "Actually, it was a gift."

The man whistled. "Nice gift."

Dominic shut the passenger door and found Ireland staring at him with a peculiar expression.

"A gift?"

"Yeah. Lisa had this delivered about a month ago."

"Seriously?"

He nodded and motioned for her to precede him toward the upper deck where Samuel had gone. "I knew nothing about it. You can only imagine how surprised I was when the doorbell rang and there it was."

"You have to tell me this story," she said as she climbed the stairs.

Dominic realized he was eye level with her behind in those cutoff shorts, and it took a moment for Ireland's request to sink in. "Uh, yeah. Of course. Lisa had taken out a life insurance policy years ago when the kids were young. After she was in a car accident. I knew that, but what I didn't know was that she'd increased the amount several times since. The note that came with the car said she knew the kids would always have what they needed but that it was my turn."

"So she picked out the car?"

"Yeah. We'd gone to a car show years ago, and I'd told her I'd have a car like that one day, once I retired or something."

"And she remembered and got it for you. That's… Wow, what a great surprise that must have been."

They'd made it to the top of the stairs, and Dominic paused to look at the view. Samuel stood at the railing and turned to wave when he spotted them. "Yeah. It was. The note she wrote informed me it was nonrefundable, nontransferable. I had to keep it and drive it and remember... I had to remember to live."

"That sounds like Lisa. I mean, from what I know of her when she was setting up the trip for you. She worried about you. How you'd... be afterwards."

Their gazes locked and he tensed at the impact. It was like Ireland saw into his soul. Saw way too much.

"Mom, look!"

Samuel pointed toward a cargo ship in the distance.

"I see it. Wonder what's on it, hmm? What do you think, Sammy?"

Dominic braced his hands against the metal rails of the ferry and gripped them until his knuckles hurt. What was he doing? Thinking? He stood there telling Ireland about his *wife* and all that Lisa had done for him... while noticing her legs and her smile and her eyes, her laugh? The way she looked in those shorts?

Where was the love, honor, and cherish in that?

Chapter 15

Something had happened.

An hour later, Ireland sat across the table from Dominic in one of Southport's popular seaside restaurants very aware that his mood had shifted with the telling of the car story.

He'd been as nice and polite as always, but there was a tension in him that hadn't been there before, and because of it, London found herself jealous of a dead woman.

How awful was that? What kind of person—what kind of friend—felt such things? Lisa was a wonderful person, obviously a loving wife and mother.

So how could she feel anything remotely close to jealousy?

But that love? That devotion and the way Dominic talked about Lisa?

She wanted that. *Craved* that.

She shoved her food around on her plate and wondered why Rich hadn't felt that way about her. Things had changed between them over the years, but wasn't that part of life? The ebb and flow of a relationship combined with work and having a child? No one stayed the same. No one could stay the same. But that commitment… vows… integrity and trust in a relationship? Those things were huge and they were supposed to last forever. But how was someone ever supposed to know for sure that the other person was as committed to them and the marriage as they were?

Was that even possible?

No. Because people were human and they'd always disappoint.

"Mom? You're not listening."

She blinked to awareness and flushed beneath the combined stares of her son and Dominic. "I'm sorry. You caught me. What did you say?"

"You were making funny faces. What were you thinking about?"

Oh, baby. That is something I can't tell you. "Just thinking about how hungry I am." She glanced at Dominic and found his stare as unsettling as she had before. "Aren't you hungry?"

Samuel nodded vigorously. "*Starving.* And I want dessert. Please," he quickly added.

"Once you eat all of your food, you'll be full."

"Maybe," he said. "But there's always room for dessert. Right, Dominic?"

Dominic smiled but she noted the amusement didn't show in his eyes like it sometimes did.

Yeah, something had definitely changed.

LATER THAT EVENING, they took the ferry back to Carolina Cove after walking a bit along Southport's beautiful waterfront.

"Lots of people out tonight."

"'Tis the season," she murmured, grateful for the tourists because it meant she kept her job and got paid. She much preferred going to the beach in the off-season, but seeing the little town so alive was fun, too.

Dominic stopped at the light and waited for it to change, and she studied his profile. He drove confidently and she felt safe with him behind the wheel. He didn't get angry at others on the road and floor the powerful car to ridiculous speeds as he passed or repeatedly change lanes like Rich had done.

She frowned at the realization she'd compared Dominic and Rich once again. On the surface, the two men were similar. Handsome, well-educated, intelligent. But inside they were as different as night and day, and she was pleased with the ability to discern the difference. It was amazing what heartbreak and experience could do to sharpen one's instincts.

The light changed and Dominic made the turn. She gathered her purse and the bag of cotton candy left over from the ball game earlier in the day and dreaded the thought of going into work tomorrow. She was tired. Worn out from the day and the tilt-a-whirl of her thoughts.

"I'll carry him inside."

She looked at Dominic in surprise and then into the backseat, only then seeing why Samuel's chatter had stopped. He'd fallen asleep, and while there was no way she could carry her almost-ten-year-old son up the stairs now, Dominic didn't think twice about it.

Seeing Sammy cradled against Dominic's broad chest left her trembling, and she turned away. Because for the first time—the very first time—since Rich had left them, she felt enough for a man to want the experi-ence of being held by him. Wanted to be cradled against him and sheltered in his arms, if only for a brief moment.

Her hands shook but she managed to open the door. The trip up yet another flight of stairs to the bedrooms left her breathless because of the awareness that Dominic followed carrying Sam, and it felt like they were a family.

She turned on the bedside lamp and quickly scooped the clothes and other items from the top of Samuel's bed, yanking the blanket low so Dominic could lay him down. Samuel was so worn out he barely stirred and simply rolled to his side and closed his glazed eyes once more.

Back in the hallway, she pulled the door mostly closed, and they made the return trip to the main level.

"You have a beautiful home. It suits you."

The compliment pleased her, but only because she'd decorated the house bit by bit since Holland's idea of decorating was to have a bed and a coffeemaker. "Thanks. It's a work in progress. Holland travels so much she told me to do what I wanted so… I have been."

She looked around the interior, trying to see it from his viewpoint, but when she glanced back at Dominic, she found his gaze rising to meet hers, as though he'd stared at her… mouth?

"I should go. It's late."

"Of course." She walked him to the door. "Thank you for everything. It was definitely a fun day. We haven't done anything like that in a while, and it was long overdue."

"For me, too."

If he hadn't said that and seemed to mean it, she could've opened the door and let him go unheeded. But he had said it, and he had seemed to mean it, and she found herself stepping forward to give him a hug goodbye even as she told herself not to.

But there she was against him, and his arms enveloped her. She closed her eyes, reveling in the warmth and strength and tightness of the embrace that didn't last nearly long enough.

She forced herself to let go and took a step back but gasped when she met his gaze. One second she stood free of him, and the next she was pressed back against the door, her head cradled in his palm, his lips on hers, searching, seeking. Gentle and rough and everything a kiss was supposed to be.

Seconds passed before he tore his mouth from hers, and a long moment passed before he gently but firmly moved her out of the way. She watched, lips tingling, as he walked out into the night and the door shut behind him with a soft thud no doubt meant not to wake her son.

"Mom? Did you just kiss Dominic?"

Chapter 16

"Hellooo? Earth to Ireland. Anybody in there?" London snapped her fingers in front of Ireland's face.

Ireland blinked and focused on her sister. "What?"

"Okay, what happened between you and Dominic yesterday?"

"What makes you think something happened?"

London tilted her head to one side and crossed her arms over her front. "You spent the entire day with him and didn't get home until late."

"How do you know that?"

"Rita Donaldson saw you having dinner in Southport with what she called 'an extremely sexy man.' Now spill."

The problem with *spilling* it to her sister was that what one knew, the others knew—and that wasn't something she was prepared to deal with just yet. "Um…"

"Hey, Mom, did you tell Aunt Londy you kissed Dominic?"

"Oooh, really? So that's the problem?"

Ireland winced at her son's big mouth and sent him

her best mama glare. "Didn't we agree we *weren't* going to say anything to anyone?"

"But Aunt London isn't anyone, she's family."

"Yeah, I'm family," London repeated with a broad grin. "So they kissed, huh, Sammy? Did it last a long time?"

"Yeah. It was gross."

Ireland buried her head in her hands with a loud groan. "Samuel, go… I don't know, do something. *Now*."

London held up her hand and stopped Samuel before he could run off. "Trash needs taken out and the coffee grounds need put in the composting bin."

"Ah, man."

"Hey, you don't work, I don't pay."

"Yes, ma'am."

"I should go. I need to—"

"Don't you dare move from that stool or I'll tie you to it."

Ireland released another groan and waited for Samuel to head off to gather the trash and do his chores for the day at London's.

"He's gone. Now tell me everything, including how my precious little Sammy was so traumatized by your make-out session."

Ireland rolled her eyes at London's description of her son's reaction and held up her decaf coffee mug. "If you want that story, you may have to add a little something to this."

London's eyebrows rose. "It was bad? *Really*? He looks like he'd be a good kisser."

"It wasn't— It was—"

"Yes?" London bent and retrieved something from the secret stash kept on hand for after hours and family gatherings and poured a bit in Ireland's coffee, making it an Irish after her namesake.

"It was a great kiss. It just shouldn't have happened."

"Why not?"

She took a long draw of the now warm coffee and enjoyed the added kick. "Because he practically ran out the door afterward and I haven't seen him since. His car was gone when I got to the inn for work, and he's been gone all day."

"He checked out?"

"No. At least, not officially."

"Then maybe he's coming back."

"Is he?"

"Did you check his room?"

"No. Oh, Londy. Maybe it *was* a bad kiss and he isn't coming back. Maybe I'm so out of practice that I don't know a good kiss from a bad one anymore. Maybe—"

"*Maybe* he just had something he wanted to do today and… forgot to mention it?"

Ireland shot her sister a disbelieving glare. "He's Lisa's husband."

"He's no one's husband. Not anymore. We've talked about this."

"But—"

"Look, Ireland, did you have a good day? Laugh, talk, have fun?"

She nodded. "We had a wonderful day. At least I thought so… right up until he stormed out of the house like he couldn't get away from me fast enough."

"Okay, so maybe it took him by surprise, too. You know? Maybe he's not there yet emotionally, but it happened?"

Ireland shook her head and took another long sip.

"It doesn't matter. He left. And he had to know after kissing me that would— That's bad form."

"Hey, cut him some slack. I'd say he's a little out of practice, too, if you know what I mean."

She lifted her head and frowned. "No. What do you mean?"

"Oh, Ireland, seriously? He was married for how many years? And she was sick for how many years? And if he's mourned as deeply as you think and as much as Lisa thought he would… then it's been a while for him, too, and he's just as freaked out as you are right now."

"I *hate it* when you make sense."

"I know. So gimme the details."

"I hope they're juicy."

They turned in unison to find Frankie walking in.

"You're just in time—"

"Can we *not*?" Ireland muttered to London.

"To hear Ireland tell us about her fantastic date with the hunky Mr. Dunn. It ended with kissing."

Frankie hiked herself up onto the stool next to Ireland. "Do tell. But you might want to wait or repeat it again. Carolina's on her way."

"Why? The shift just started a half hour ago."

Frankie shrugged. "I dunno. Said she needs a break and it's slow, so she's closing the office for a half hour. Did you already tell her?"

"No."

Frankie waved a hand toward London's cell phone. "Call Holland and put her on speaker."

Ireland groaned and took another long pull from the Irish coffee. This right here? This was reason number 484 why she wasn't ready for dating.

Chapter 17

"So you're back."

Dominic looked up from where he sat outside the inn's office, waiting on it to reopen, and found Carolina staring at him from several feet away. His gut knotted at the expression she wore. "The sign says you should've reopened a half hour ago."

"Sister emergency."

He winced at the news. "I take it you know?"

"That you stormed out after kissing Ireland? Oh, yeah." She pulled keys from the pocket of her flowy skirt and closed the distance to the door.

"How is she?"

"Why don't you ask her yourself?"

He rubbed a hand over his head to his neck and squeezed hard. "I thought she'd be here."

"Nope. She's gone for the day."

"Look, I don't expect you to understand but—"

"*But* you still love your wife yet you're drawn to Ireland and gave in to a moment of weakness. Am I right?"

"That… sums it up, yeah."

"I thought so. It's really not that difficult to understand."

Dominic followed her into the small lobby of the inn. "I'm going to apologize."

"Good." She grinned at him over her shoulder as she rounded the check-in counter. "That means you're handsome *and* smart. Good on you, mate."

He laughed at her choice of words. "Did you suddenly turn Australian?"

"Nope. Just practicing for when I go there this winter. I work as much as I can through the tourist season so I can travel in the off months."

"Alone?" He'd had a hard enough time coming to the inn for a two-week vacation. He couldn't imagine traveling the world as a single. Experiences like that were meant to be shared.

"Mostly. Sometimes I meet other people along the way and we'll travel part of the way together. It just depends."

Carolina was definitely the free spirit of the sisters he'd met. "Women alone are often targets. Keep your guard up." He felt the need to add the warning, especially seeing as how she wasn't that much older than his daughter.

"Will do, Daddy-O. So, how are you going to apologize to Ireland?"

He ignored her sarcasm and focused on the real issue. "I don't know." On the way back to Carolina Cove, he'd thought about picking up a bouquet of flowers, but that was something he would've done for Lisa after an argument. With Ireland… he wasn't sure what was appropriate.

"Well, is it an apology for leaving, or for kissing her?"

Dominic added blunt to the list of characteristics Carolina possessed. "I don't know."

"Interesting. You know you could've called from Atlanta to apologize. You didn't have to come all the way back here for that."

Yes, he could have. But calling hadn't felt right, either. He wanted to make sure Ireland was okay. Wanted to… somehow make it right.

"Want some advice?"

He leaned heavily against the counter and wiped a hand roughly over his face. "At this stage, it certainly couldn't hurt."

"Hmm. Well, you might not like it, but you and Ireland are both stuck in the past."

"I'm not stuck."

"Oh? It's been a year—no offense—and you're freaked out over kissing a beautiful, single, wonderful woman. That's not moving forward, that's stuck."

"There's more to it than that."

"How so?"

"I shouldn't have taken advantage. I ruined a good day with my behavior."

"Did you ruin it, though?"

He narrowed his gaze on Carolina. "Why do you ask that? Did she say something to you?"

"Maybe. She wasn't happy that you left. She's totally ticked, actually, but the funny thing is, she didn't seem all that upset about the kissing. Just the leaving."

So Ireland hadn't minded the kiss? "She told me she isn't ready to date."

"But she went on one—with you."

"That was for Samuel."

"Hmm. Maybe. But I think she's more worried that *you're* not ready to date," Carolina countered.

"I'm not sure that I am."

"Ah. But you went to the game, had a nice time, and ended said night with a kiss you initiated before you got all weirded out."

"Is there a point to this?"

"I'm getting there. Ready?" She waited on his nod. "Look, Ireland's ex did a number on her trust level, and while our dad's a great example that not all men are cheating liars, it might help Ireland to have a male *friend* who's actually just a good guy. Not ready to date? Fine. Then be that friend for her while you're here. The rest will fall into place if it's supposed to."

Was it really that simple? Could it be that simple? Was he putting too much pressure on himself to be something Ireland hadn't asked him to be? Didn't expect him to be?

There's only one way to find out.

AN HOUR LATER, Dominic was beginning to think Carolina had warned Ireland of his return and she wasn't coming home because of it.

He paced the length of the screened porch and found himself in front of a photo of all of the sisters together, smiling at the camera. The girls were young, Ireland in her early teens at most. Three of the five sported braces, and all of them had a smattering of freckles across their noses.

A sharp gasp caught his attention. He'd been so deep in thought he hadn't heard Ireland ascending the stairs to the screened porch. He'd debated the wisdom of entering without an invitation, but waiting outside had become impossible when the mosquitoes began making a meal out of him.

"You're... back."

So Carolina hadn't warned her sister. "Can I come in?"

She hesitated a long moment but then moved to unlock the main door of the house. He followed her inside.

"Frankie's dropping Samuel off in a little bit after a Mario Brothers match. You probably shouldn't be here when he gets home. Sammy... saw us."

He winced at the news and lifted a hand, rubbed it roughly over his face. "I'm sorry. I shouldn't have done that—kissed you. I don't know what I was thinking. You've made it perfectly clear you're not ready to date and... I crossed the line."

"It's fine, Dominic."

"It's not fine. You're upset."

"No. I mean, yeah, maybe I was, a little, because of how you left. But I understand."

"I doubt you do." She stared up at him, her eyes widening a bit at his tone. But how could she possibly understand what he was having such a hard time coming to grips with himself?

Because the truth?

Carolina was right. He'd initiated that kiss. *Wanted* to kiss Ireland and had pretty much the entire day. But the thought of a relationship and his kids' reactions... And then there was Samuel to consider...

"Explain it to me then."

Such a simple command. Such a complicated and involved answer. "We'd... had a wonderful day together.

More fun than I've had in years. So when we got back here and you looked at me with those big blue eyes of yours… it seemed like the thing to do."

"So why did you leave? Where did you go?"

He turned, needing some room, when he found himself gazing into her eyes once more. He didn't remember a time in his life when he'd felt so divided. "I started back to Atlanta—"

"Oh." She dropped her purse and the bag she carried onto the dining table.

"I didn't get very far. I wound up walking for miles at some outdoor mall in Myrtle Beach before I turned around and drove back here. I went to the office first, but you'd already left for the day. Carolina said you were at London's talking with all of the sisters. Should I be scared?"

A wry smile formed on her lips. "Maybe just a little of Frankie."

"I'll keep an eye out."

"Dominic, why did you come back?"

He met her gaze and fought the frustration gnawing at his insides. Why was this so difficult? Be a friend. Have fun. Enjoy the moment. See what happens? "If I'm honest, I don't know how I feel about what happened."

"You're freaked out by it."

"Yeah, I am. It felt… wrong."

"Because of Lisa. I get it. I don't imagine this is easy for you but… it was just a kiss, right? So all's forgiven. Forget it."

Yeah, that wasn't going to happen. Not when he couldn't get her out of his head and not when… "Samuel saw us?"

"He woke up enough for a trip to the bathroom and… yeah."

Which meant the kid had probably added even more pressure to whatever it was Ireland felt in regard to that kiss. "I'll talk to him. Try to explain."

"I tried to but… he thinks we're dating now. That yesterday was a date and that's why… If we both say we're just friends and leave it at that, maybe he'll understand and drop it."

"Are we? Friends?" He read the wariness in her gaze. His question brought up her emotional barriers due to the way her shoulders lifted toward her ears.

"Of course. It was a mistake but it won't happen again, right? You're still mourning, and if I'm going to be in a relationship, I'm certainly not going to complicate it by making it a long-distance one. Relationships are hard enough without adding that to the mix."

"So now you're ready to date?"

"Yeah. Yeah, I've decided that I am. I did a lot of thinking after you left. That kiss made me realize how much I miss being a couple and having someone to talk to and share things with. I mean, that kiss was nice and it—"

"Nice?" She blinked up at him as though in confusion, and although he told himself the critique didn't matter, he had to know. "The kiss was… *nice*."

"Um… yeah. What? Why are you looking at me like… Nice is not an insult."

Of course it was an insult. No man wanted his kisses to be *nice*.

"What else could it be when you took off out of here like your heels were on fire? The point was it made me think and… Dominic, why are you staring at me like that?"

"We need to practice."

"I'm sorry, what?"

"You heard me."

"Practice? K-kissing?"

"Dating." Though the other was an intriguing idea as well.

"Practice dating?"

He liked the fact that his suggestion flustered her. "Someone mentioned to me that I should consider a practice date with a friend. A friend who knows my situation and understands. You just said you do."

"Well, yes, I do, but—"

"And earlier Carolina informed me that you and I both live in the past. I'm beginning to think she's right."

"You talked to Carolina? About *dating*?"

"I did. She had some good advice."

"Seriously?"

He laughed at Ireland's surprise. "She told me to be a friend to you and suggested we hang out together while I'm here. Then there's no pressure for either of us."

"And the practice dating idea?"

"That came from someone else but it makes sense, right? Maybe we should give dating a test drive."

"Um…"

"You said you're ready."

"Well, yeah, but you are—"

"A friend… in need of a friend. We both now know where we stand, right? You don't want a long-distance relationship, and I'll be returning to Atlanta when my time here is up. I'm not sure I'm ready to date, but this would be a good way to test the waters and break the ice, right? It's a perfect idea."

"I dunno about *perfect*."

"Ireland, let me take you out on a legitimate date."

She stared at him a long, hard-to-breathe moment. "Are you *sure* about this?"

"No. I think we'd agree that neither one of us is entirely sure. But we both want to move forward."

"That's true."

"Ireland, you don't want your first attempt at dating again to be with some jerk. That'll discourage you and leave you right where you are now, and I need to sharpen some rusty skills so…"

"We practice on each other." This time she said it with a little more enthusiasm.

"What do you say, Ireland? Will you go out with me?" Dominic waited for her response. Watched as her teeth sank into her lip for a moment while she pondered the pros and cons. He could practically see her mind whirling, the wheels cranking.

"If you're sure you want to do this, I guess it couldn't hurt."

"That's encouraging." A smile formed on her lips, drawing his gaze.

"Hey, you get what you get. I can't say I'm not nervous about how this will work. Especially after what happened last night. Speaking of which, we need ground rules for this plan of yours."

He liked her spunk. "What do you propose?"

"Flirting is okay."

"Opening car doors, compliments, holding hands?"

She nodded. "That's approved, too."

"What about kissing?" There. He put it out there.

"Because while it took me by surprise last night, I… enjoyed it. Immensely. To me, it was better than… nice."

He loved the flush of color that entered her cheeks and parted her beautiful lips so she could take a deeper breath.

"What if we take that on a case-by-case basis," he said before she had the chance to negate kissing entirely. "After all, we're adults and perfectly capable of controlling ourselves."

After another long stare from her beautiful searching eyes, she swallowed hard, the sound audible.

"I suppose that would be okay. Case by case, I mean. But there will be no friends-with-benefits type thing. That's not me."

"Thank God. I'm pleased to hear it," he said, moving closer to where she stood. He held up his hands as if in surrender. "So, we have the rules for our little adventure?"

"For now. We can add or adjust as needed."

He held out his hand and waited for her to place her palm in his. "Deal. Carolina mentioned she would fill in for you anytime at the inn. If this conversation worked out and… we decided to do something."

"Um, yeah. Carolina is always up for extra hours, so getting coverage isn't a problem."

"Good. Tomorrow then."

"Tomorrow? Uh, okay. Wait, what are we doing? What should I wear?"

He liked hearing that question from her. "I'll let you know in the morning. I'll pick you up here around ten."

"Sammy—"

"Isn't invited this time," he told her firmly. "Carolina also said she and your other sisters would watch him."

Ireland placed her hands on her hips and sent him a disgruntled look. "You've done an awful lot of chatting with Carolina."

"She made the offer when she told me she'd help me plan a date if something happened to change our minds." Truth be told, he'd nodded his agreement to *think* about Carolina's offer before leaving the inn's office, but he was pretty sure Ireland's sister would have a date planned before he got back there to verbalize his actual acceptance of it. When combined with an idea or two of his own, he figured it would be a good, toe-dipping first attempt.

"I'm not sure I like this."

He crossed the threshold onto the deck but turned to face her. "Too late to back out now. Sweet dreams, Ireland."

Chapter 18

The following morning, Ireland paced the screened-in porch and prayed for calm while she waited for Dominic to arrive.

His instructions had been to *dress for a day of fun at the beach but bring a change of clothes for a nice dinner.*

The low, thrumming sound of the Porsche's engine filled the air, and she peeked down to see him pulling in. Her heart rate soared, and she felt like a teenager awaiting her first date ever rather than a thirty-year-old woman.

She quietly entered the house because she didn't want to seem too eager or impatient and wound up, standing behind the kitchen island as though it would protect her from the onslaught of emotions. Was she ready for this? Dating?

Dating with rules. There's a difference.

"Ireland? Okay to come in?" Dominic knocked softly on the open door.

"Yeah. Of course." He wore swim trunks and boat shoes, and a bright blue T-shirt stretched across his broad chest and hinted at muscle no desk jockey should have. He'd been in the sun quite a bit since his arrival, and it had darkened his face and arms to a honey-brown. The hints of gray mixed in with his dark brown hair sparkled in the sunlight filtering in from the windows, making him a bona fide hunk. "Um, hi."

"Good morning. You look beautiful."

"Thank you. You don't look so bad yourself." She hoped that didn't sound as cheesy as it had to her ears. Oh, why was this so awkward? Wasn't it supposed to be easier because they already knew each other? Had already kissed?

Maybe Dominic was right. Maybe they did need some practice, and who better to practice on than someone she found handsome and kind but seemingly as limited in experience due to his twenty years with Lisa? Plus, there was the fact it could only go so far since he'd be leaving to return to his regular life soon. That made him… safe. In a sense.

Actually, it kinda made him the perfect date, because if things went badly, she wouldn't have to see him at all once he returned to Atlanta.

Way to go thinking positive.

Maybe it did seem a bit negative, but the more she thought about it, the more Dominic's suggestion made perfect sense. Neither one of them had any expectations of the future because they lived two very different lives in two very different states. They were simply enjoying the moment and a beautiful summer day and… each other's company. Where was the harm in that?

She leaned over to pick up her bag from the couch and noted Dominic's eyes in the general direction of her legs. She'd caught him looking at her legs the day of the ball game, too, and felt herself flush with awareness. It wasn't like she could take credit for her long limbs seeing as how they were a gift from God, but right now she was pleased by the fact Dominic seemed to appreciate the sight of them.

She'd gone through her entire wardrobe, debating what to wear, and finally settled on a bright turquoise two-piece. Over that she had on a white tank top, khaki shorts with rolled cuffs, and a white sheer blouse half-tucked. She'd twisted her long hair in a messy knot at her nape and wore a fedora-style hat for some extra shade. In her oversize beach bag, she had the requisite towel and sunscreen but also a flirty little black dress, strappy sandals, and other necessities to freshen up and change into later. "Ready. Are you going to tell me where we're going?"

Dominic smiled at her, and she'd be lying if she said she didn't feel a flutter in her stomach as a result. Oh, he was a looker.

"It's a surprise. Let's go."

HER SURPRISE WAS INDEED a surprise and something she'd wanted to do since moving to the island two years ago but hadn't taken the time.

Ireland laughed as the wind caught her hat and nearly removed it. She quickly placed her hand atop her head to hold it in place and faced the wind as the ferry approached the docking area of Bald Head Island.

The beautiful island had a no-car rule, and as she and Dominic gathered their belongings and exited the ferry, they searched for the sign leading to the golf cart rental. In short order, they were loaded up and on their way.

"So what's first, official reader of the map?"

She stared down at the map in question, getting her bearings. "There are a few trails we can take while we head toward the market for snacks. By then we'll be hungry. But Old Baldy is just a little ways away. Go there first?"

"Sounds like a plan to me."

He made a left out of the rental area, and off they went, taking the first left they came to. They parked the golf cart and took a few pictures of the lighthouse from the outside before beginning the climb to the top. After more photos of the view, they climbed back into the cart to go again.

"Oh, how beautiful."

Dominic slowed the cart and glanced at her. "Think it's open?"

"We could find out." She bit her lip, hoping he wouldn't get impatient with her wanting to make another stop so soon, but the chapel was so beautiful from the outside, so she could only imagine what the inside looked like.

He pulled off and parked once more, and together they entered the church property, pausing along the brick-lined walkway to take in the simple beauty of the painted gray church with its gabled rooflines and arched windows flanked by white shutters. A massive tree on the right shaded much of the front lawn as well as a walkway that led to a handicapped ramp on the side.

They entered the chapel through the arched doorway, and Ireland inhaled the scent of wood and polish.

Massive stained wooden beams lined the interior ceiling and expanse of the white church. "Wow."

"Yeah," Dominic whispered, seemingly as awestruck as she was.

He moved down the aisle and continued to stare up at the wooden beams soaring into a peak beneath the steeple.

"It's breathtaking. Every church should be this beautiful."

She moved throughout the church, took lots of photos, and hoped her battery would last until the end of the day considering this was only their second stop. She closed the screen and turned to find Dominic seated on the first pew. He sat with his elbows on his knees, hands clasped loosely in front of him. Praying?

She couldn't see his face but got that impression, so she stepped into the pew closest to her and sat there in silence, letting the peace of the church calm her chaotic thoughts into a prayer of her own.

After a few minutes, Dominic stood and faced her and she smiled at him. "Ready for the next stop?"

"Whenever you are."

They continued on their golf cart journey, pausing here and there at pull-offs to read the island markers and take in the history of the barrier island. Since they were nearing the middle of the island, where the shops and market were located, they stopped yet again to get supplies for the beach.

Dominic picked up various trinkets and items to check them out, and she shook her head at his antics when he pulled the trigger of a goofy-looking shark's head. It made the shark's mouth open and release, and Dominic approached her with an ornery grin, moving the toy up her arm and shoulder onto her neck as it nipped at her.

"Think Samuel would like this?"

Her heart melted at Dominic's thoughtfulness, but she shook her head. "He has at least three of them. Thank you, though."

Dominic replaced the toy into the bin, and they moved on through the store, taking their time browsing the selections of souvenirs as well as food supplies and drinks.

They bought hummus and chips, some apples, water, and other supplies to go into the cooler Carolina had provided Dominic and made their way to the cashier.

"I've been watching you shop," the older lady told them. "You two are the cutest couple. Have you been together long?"

"Uh…" She looked to Dominic for an appropriate reply and saw him wink at the cashier.

"It's our first date."

"Oh! Well, I hope you enjoy our little island."

"We intend to."

With those three little words, Dominic put a blush on her cheeks that had the lady smiling at Ireland and giving her a knowing look.

They left the building, and Dominic caught her hand and held it.

"I don't remember the last time I've seen a woman blush. I like it."

"It… uh, comes with the red hair, I guess." Her insides fluttered and left her trembling. How was it possible Dominic could do that to her with a look? A touch? She blamed the day and proximity and no small amount of nerves.

Back on the golf cart, they continued their tour of the island, chatting about people and plants and even the dogs they saw along the way, and the fact that Rocco had become a regular visitor at London's coffee shop, coming and going at will the last several days.

"Look at the water," Dominic murmured.

"Wow. It's so blue today."

Dominic slowed the golf cart and turned toward her, using one long finger to gently tug her sunglasses to the tip of her nose. "Mmm, I thought so. The water matches your eyes."

He seemed to study them, and she found herself holding her breath, wondering if he was going to make a case for kissing. Wondering if she wanted him to, just to see if the second experience would be as good as the first, or if the trembling she felt inside could be chalked up entirely as nerves.

A short ring of a bike bell behind them alerted them to someone else on the cart path, and Dominic lifted his hand in greeting as a man on a bike passed, followed by a woman.

The moment lost, Ireland tamped down her curiosity and more than a little disappointment as Dominic got the cart moving again.

Chapter 19

Dominic shook the water from his head and wiped at his eyes as he emerged from the surf on South Beach several hours later. They'd toured the island via the golf cart, climbed to the top of Old Baldy Lighthouse, visited the church, and held hands while walking along the nature trails.

They ate a picnic lunch beneath an umbrella that shielded them from all but the most aggressive of seagulls, and now Ireland sunbathed in a modest two-piece that boggled his mind and required a swim to distract himself from those long legs of hers and the fact that he'd almost kissed her less than an hour into their date when he'd stopped the cart to look at the ocean.

He made his way up the beach and lowered himself onto the massive beach towel beside her to dry out. The chairs were beneath the umbrella shade and more comfortable, but he liked being able to turn his head and see her. Limiting his vision and focusing on her face rather than the beautiful length of her stretched out for the sun wasn't such a bad thing, either.

"Did you have a nice swim?"

The corners of his mouth lifted at her muffled question. She sounded sleepy and it was adorable. "Yeah. You should come in."

"I don't do the ocean."

A huff of a laugh left him. "How do you not *do* the ocean? You live at the beach."

She lifted her head enough to prop her cheek on her folded arms. "It's pretty simple, actually. I *love* the beach, walking along the shore, fishing, and boating, but I don't swim in the ocean. That's for the fish—and the sharks. I like pools, where I can see what's swimming with me."

He rolled to his side and propped himself up, giving in to the temptation of enjoying the view. "Anything else you don't do?"

"Skydive. Planes and flying are fine, but jumping out of a perfectly good plane makes no sense at all."

"Mm. On that we agree. What else?"

"Raw sushi. Have you seen the videos of those tapeworms they've found?"

He chuckled as he lowered himself again and rolled onto his back, closing his eyes behind his sunglasses.

"What do you like to do in Atlanta?"

"I'm pretty boring. I work. A lot. Once L—" Realizing he was about to be that guy on a date reminiscing about his late wife, he stopped himself.

"Dominic, you can talk about her. It's okay."

"No, it's not. Lisa isn't fun, first-date conversation."

"Yeah, well, I think we both agree we're beyond that, and today isn't normal for either of us, practice date or not. Besides, we're not kids. Adults have a little more to deal with baggage-wise, and it has to surface sometime."

She'd removed her sunglasses to lie on her stomach

and used her hat to shade her eyes. Now he stared into the depths and fought the battle between his guilt over Lisa and intrigue for the woman beside him. "That may be true, but you deserve a man's full attention, Ireland. Don't ever forget that."

Her eyes brightened in color, and it took him a moment to realize it was from tears. She blinked rapidly and shoved herself upright, onto her knees, lashes low over her eyes while she readjusted her hat and found her sunglasses. "Thank you. For saying that. I didn't feel that way in my marriage. Once the novelty wore off, his interests were always elsewhere." She brushed the sand from her thighs. "There. See? Now you're not the only one talking about our pasts on a date."

"Time for a change of subject then. How about a stroll on the beach since you don't get in the water?"

"Are you sure you're not going to drag me in once we get there?"

He got to his feet and held out his hands to help her up, liking the feel of her palms in his and the way she fit against his side when he pulled her close. "Guess we'll have to wait and find out."

THEY SPENT the rest of the afternoon on the beach, sitting beneath the umbrella talking about everything from favorite sports teams to favorite foods and pet peeves and dozing a bit before taking another stroll along the water's edge.

"Time to go," he said as they approached their spot.

"Mmm. I hate for the day to end. It's been so nice."

Ireland's eyes widened when he growled at her and used an old high school wrestling move to take her—

gently—down to the towel. "*Nice*? Is that the only word you know?"

He tickled her, and she laughed, head back, gasping for air, hands grasping at his to try to still them.

"Okay! I'm sorry! Uncle!"

He planted his hands on either side of her shoulders and leaned low. "Today has been better than nice. Admit it."

She breathed heavily from the tickling, and he'd have to be blind not to be aware of her chest rising and falling from the exertion or the way she smiled up at him. "It's been *wonderful*, Dominic. Thank you for insisting I allow you to be my first date."

He wanted to kiss her. He had the feeling she wanted him to kiss her, but the beach was summer-season crowded, and he'd never been one for PDAs, so he suppressed the desire to take initiative. "Come on. Let's get moving. We can't be late."

"You have a reservation?"

"Something like that."

"Oh, but I need to stop somewhere and change."

"We can do that there."

"Where? On the ferry?"

He stood and pulled her to her feet once more. "So many questions. Don't ruin the surprise. You'll see."

Thirty minutes later, they returned the rented golf cart, and Dominic watched Ireland's expression change from confusion to one of sheer pleasure when she spotted the captain of a rather large yacht waving at them.

"We're going on *that*? Really?"

"I called in a favor from a client who always offers

the use of it if I was ever in the area. We can shower and change on board."

"Where's it taking us for dinner?"

He loved her enthusiasm and the excited smile she wore. "You'll see."

"You're not going to tell me? Seriously?"

She reached out and grasped his hand in hers, her other hand sliding over his forearm and squeezing. He smiled down at her. "It won't be a surprise if I do, and I'm beginning to realize you love surprises."

"I do. This is amazing," she said, hugging his arm to her body and pressing her face against his biceps while she peeked up at him. "This is the *nicest* practice date ever."

Chapter 20

Ireland inhaled and held the salt air in her lungs for a long moment before releasing it, trying to still the frantic beating of her heart.

Practice dating was dangerous for her equilibrium.

Throughout the day, she'd laughed and flirted and talked with Dominic. He had proven himself to be intelligent, articulate, not to mention funnier and more playful than she'd thought a stuffy patent attorney might be.

Now after a shower and slipping into the dress she'd brought with her, she wondered how wise it had been to accept Dominic's invitation. Because this Dominic? The Dominic she'd seen and experienced firsthand today was someone she could fall for. And how stupid would that be to fall for a *friend* still mourning his *wife*? A friend who would *leave* when his stay was over.

Was it even possible to fall for someone so quickly? "Breathe," she whispered. "It's a practice date, not a real one."

"Are you talking to yourself or the sunset?"

Dominic emerged from the boat's interior, his hair wet but neat, a short-sleeved polo clinging to his broad shoulders. He'd exchanged the swim shorts and tee for khaki slacks and looked very much the successful Atlanta law partner that he was. "Myself."

"And you were saying?"

She shivered in the breeze and caught her breath when Dominic noticed and slid his warm hands down her arms from shoulder to elbow and back up again, sharing his warmth. "Just something I need to remember," she whispered. His skills didn't seem all that rusty to her.

"The crew has dinner ready on the top deck. Are you hungry?" He stepped back and held out his hand.

Ireland let him lead the way to the stairs. Along the way, she picked up the sweater she'd brought with her to combat the breeze.

On the upper deck, a string of lights twinkled overhead, soft music played from an unseen speaker, and dinner consisted of a salad and shrimp scampi and a rich, smooth wine.

Like earlier today, they discussed general topics. The latest books and movies, events taking place the upcoming weekend. She asked more questions about his kids and told stories from Samuel's school year that left Dominic laughing so hard his eyes watered.

"That kid could rule the world one day."

"I know, right? But it's just so *normal* for him. I listen to some moms talk about their kids playing video games all day, every day, and I can't help but think they're so boring. Oh, my— I shouldn't have said that. That's an awful thing to say about someone's child."

"No, you're right. At least he's active and involved.

And Samuel is a good kid. That's the most important thing."

Ireland held her wineglass to her lips and sipped, unable to wrap her mind around the day. It would definitely go down as the most romantic date she'd ever been on, but it also made her wonder how others would ever compare. Today would be hard to top both in location and company.

"Look."

Dominic pointed a finger and she gasped. The sunny blue sky had faded to reds and oranges and deep, deep purples while they'd eaten, and now the sun's last rays filled the horizon with spectacular color.

"The red makes me think of your hair. When the sun hits it a certain way, your hair turns fiery."

"My mom's a redhead, too, so there's definitely plenty in the mix."

"How did your parents meet?"

"My dad was stationed overseas and my mom was studying abroad for the summer. She was having coffee at a bistro and he walked by. They both swear it was love at first sight."

"You don't believe in that?"

"Do you?" she countered, not sure she wanted to answer that since the original question involved her parents and no child of any age wanted to visualize their parents in the alternative lust-at-first-sight stage.

"Certain aspects, yeah."

"Really?"

"You sound surprised."

She gazed out at the water, pondering his words. "I guess I shouldn't be. At least not anymore. You didn't strike me as romantic, but after today, you most definitely qualify."

"Was it too much?"

Her denial was automatic and truthful. "No. No, it was perfect. A woman would have to be crazy not to enjoy a day like today."

"Does that mean you'd consider trying it again?"

Another date? With Dominic? "Um, yeah. Of course. P-practice makes perfect. Isn't that the saying?"

The music playing on the speaker changed to a slow song, and she watched as Dominic scooted his chair back and stood, holding out his hand to her.

"Shall we?"

And he dances, too?

She was wearing her flat, strappy sandals, her head barely coming to his chin, and she loved the way his height made her feel small and feminine.

Dominic pulled her into his arms beneath the twinkling lights, beginning a slow dance that stole what was left of her defenses. *Enjoy the time like Carolina says. Be in the moment. If it happens, it happens.* "Dominic?"

"Mm?"

"Lisa was blessed to have you as a husband."

He tugged her closer and lowered his lips so that they brushed her ear. She shivered, tilting her head so that her cheek slid against the five-o'clock shadow of his chin. A non-kiss that was as close as you could get to a kiss without actually kissing.

"Your husband was a fool."

Chapter 21

"You're falling in love with him," Holland said a week later, her words carried away by the wind.

Falling?

As hard as it was to believe, it was too late for that. She'd fall*en*. Like all of the hooks, lines, and sinkers tossed off the pier into the water below. She'd jumped in with both feet and was still sinking.

Ireland sat on the beach between London and Frankie, who had lain back on the sand. It was late, going on midnight, and the lights of the pier and the moon up above danced atop the rolling waves as they crashed ashore. Carolina and Holland sat opposite them, backs to the water and worried expressions revealed by the moonlight.

Dominic had dropped her off at the house, and she'd stepped inside to find Holland had returned. Her sister had taken one look at her and sent a quick text to the rest of the sisters to meet at "their spot."

A little ways down the beach from the pier house and inn was a mailbox labeled Dream Catcher. The beach near that mailbox had become their place from the moment their parents had moved onto the island with five emotional girls in tow who needed a place to express themselves. Over the years, it had held more than a few of their anonymous notes.

"Wait, where's Sammy?" London asked.

"Sleepover at a friend's house," Holland said.

"Ireland? Is she right? Are you falling for him?" Frankie asked, rising up to her elbows to stare at her.

"I told Carolina it was a bad idea," London said, shaking her head.

"It's not her fault." It was hers. She had broken the unspoken rule of practice dating.

"I had a feeling this would happen. You were too vulnerable to handle that. Besides, a date's a date."

And they'd gone on them. Every single day of Dominic's stay. Sometimes with Sammy, sometimes alone. They'd gone to a pickup game and cheered Dominic on from behind the fence. Attended church at the pavilion and fished the pier again. Toured the *Battleship North Carolina* and stayed in town, wandering around the historic district. They'd gone to the aquarium, had lunch and dinner at various restaurants around Wilmington, walked the river walk, and danced to the live music. Held hands and strolled along the shore with the waves rolling over their bare feet. Walked out to the T and gazed silently into the distance. It was those quiet moments she'd miss the most. The ones where no words were needed or necessary.

"What are you going to do?"

The lump in Ireland's throat choked her, and she didn't take her gaze off of the water in response to Carolina's question. She gazed at the waves crashing onto the shore, tumbling the shells and sand until it receded back into the ocean like the wave had never happened. Dominic would leave, go back to Atlanta. *Like nothing had ever happened.* She cleared her throat and blinked away the sting of tears she blamed on the wind. "Nothing."

"What? You're not going to *tell* him how you feel?" London placed her hand on Ireland's arm. "Ireland?"

The touch broke her out of her trance, and Ireland cleared her throat and focused. "No. Of course not. Dominic is… vulnerable. Telling him would pressure him, take advantage of him, in the worst way. It's my decision," she said to London. "And if any of you say anything to him, I will throttle you," she said to Carolina, "like I did when we were little and you read my diary. I won't do that to him," she said to Holland. "So you're not to say a single word," she said to Frankie. "Dominic and I agreed to hang out. We had rules and he's kept them. He… hasn't even kissed me again, because we agreed to take it a moment at a time, and obviously he hasn't felt moved to. He's leaving tomorrow. I've known him two weeks. I'm not even sure it's possible to fall in love in two weeks."

"But you did," Carolina said softly.

"And Mom and Dad did," Holland added. "It's possible if he's the right man for you."

The right man? Did they even exist? She was too afraid of getting her hopes up, too afraid of believing Dominic might feel the same for her as she did for him to consider taking that kind of risk.

The way she felt now? Here? This was him not knowing. Not responding. This overwhelming, stomach-churning, sick feeling inside of her was better than watching him leave her *aware* that she loved him. She wasn't sure she could survive that happening a second time.

"When are you going to give him the letter?" London asked.

The other sisters looked at London in confusion before turning toward her, but Ireland supposed it didn't matter now if they knew. "I'll give him Lisa's letter when he checks out tomorrow. Just like she asked me to do."

Frankie slipped her arm through Ireland's and leaned her head against her right shoulder. London did the same on the left, while Holland and Carolina scooted forward on the sand and enveloped her legs until they were all connected.

Ireland kept her eyes on the water, blinking hard, head tilted back to inhale the salt air as she drew strength from them to face what came with the sunrise.

They sat there for a long time without moving, without talking. "We need to get back," she murmured after a while. "We have church in the morning."

One by one, they got to their feet, brushed the sand from their clothes, and turned for the walk back. Ireland waited before she pulled the hastily written Post-it from her pocket. She opened the lid of the mailbox and tucked it into the back. *Catch that, Dream Catcher.*

Chapter 22

Dominic loaded his suitcase into the Porsche and battled the war raging inside of him. He wasn't sure when it had happened, but sometime during the last few weeks, his thinking changed from wondering if he was ready to date to wanting his practice dates with Ireland to be the real deal. The lasting, this-could-grow-into-something kind of real that blended families and began another family tree.

As it always did, guilt surfaced, because his marriage to Lisa had been a good one. A loving one. They'd had their share of arguments over the years but nothing that ever made them want to toss in the towel. Marriage was something to be taken seriously. Vows were meant to be revered, and both he and Lisa had worked hard to keep that commitment to each other strong.

But she wasn't here any longer, and he found himself craving that kind of relationship again. The laughter and fun, the companionship of a wonderful, loving woman.

The trip to Bald Head Island had ended with the

yacht dropping them off at a marina in Carolina Cove. He'd walked Ireland home, her hand in his, and left her at the door with a hug when he'd wanted so much more.

There were women he could date. There had always been women offering to comfort him after Lisa's death, but he hadn't been the slightest bit interested. Until Ireland.

But what could he offer her when she'd made it clear she didn't want a long-distance relationship? He was due back to work in Atlanta on Monday. His two weeks there had gone by slowly at first, but after their first practice date, the days hadn't lasted long enough, while the nights had lasted too long. Time he'd spent staring up at the ceiling in his hotel room or sitting on his balcony watching the waves while trying to come to grips with whatever was happening to him. Between them.

"Mom's sad, you know."

He looked up and met Samuel's direct gaze. "I know. I am, too. I'm going to miss you."

Samuel's chin quivered for a moment before he scrunched his face up and took off running.

"Samuel!"

The kid kept going, and Dominic mentally kicked himself once more. Ireland might have agreed to their friendship and practice dates, but Samuel had been a part of a few of them and was now hurting because of it.

He turned toward the office door and saw Ireland standing in the doorway. She closed and locked the door, the sign in the window stating the office would reopen in an hour after church and listing an emergency number.

"I'll talk to Sammy," she said as she approached, not quite meeting his gaze. "He'll be fine. My dad will distract him when they get back. They'll be here tomorrow so it's… it's all good."

"I never meant to hurt him—or you. You know that, right?"

"Of course." Ireland glanced at a couple walking by on the sidewalk. "Drive safe, Dominic."

He lifted his hand and brushed the hair from her mouth, tucked it behind her ear. "I saw you walking with your sisters on the beach last night. I wanted to call out but I didn't want to intrude."

"We were just… talking. Holland's home."

"I would've liked to have met her."

Ireland's face was tilted up as she talked to him, and he reached out once more, snagging her sunglasses and gently removing them.

"Dominic…"

"Let me see you." He tucked the sunglasses atop her head for safekeeping and framed her face in his palms. "I would very much like to kiss you good—"

The words had barely left his mouth when she launched herself toward him, meeting his lips with a kiss that rocked him to his soul. Sweet and innocent, heady and mind-blowing, it melded lips and tongues and breath and expressed everything he couldn't. A whimper escaped her, and he used his hold to gently turn her, press her against his car. He deepened the kiss to one that wasn't sweet or innocent at all but revealed everything the last two weeks of knowing her had meant to him. Even though he couldn't say it.

After a long, long moment, Ireland ended the kiss, her grip on his arms tight, until she slowly let go. "Drive s-safe."

Dominic slid his hand beneath her chin and lifted

her face, hoping she would meet his gaze, but she didn't. "Ireland…"

"Here. This is for you," she whispered, the words thick with tears.

"Ireland, you don't have to give me anything."

"It's not from me."

She shoved an envelope toward him.

"She said to tell you it's the last one. Goodbye, Dominic."

Ireland slipped from between him and the car and hurried down the street toward the pavilion. Dominic turned the envelope over, recognizing his name written in Lisa's handwriting.

The envelope crumpled in his fist, and he threw the wad into the passenger seat of his car before climbing behind the wheel.

He started the engine. Then just as quickly punched the button to turn it off. He glared at the envelope and growled as he reached for it, then ripped it open.

Dear Dominic…

IRELAND DIDN'T SIT beneath the pavilion like she usually did on Sundays but instead found a nearby swing where she could listen to the service while staring at the ocean. She needed peace, and the sunlight flickering atop the water like diamonds, the sound of the waves, and the words preached behind her, reminding her of God's grace, were what held her together through moments like this, while Samuel silently cried for them both.

Seconds after she'd sat down, Samuel had joined her, plopping down on the swing beside her and burrowing into her side like he had as a baby. They sat huddled together, silent, and after a while, the service ended and the crowd dispersed. She leaned over and kissed her son's head. "We're going to be okay."

"But he's gone."

"Sammy, honey, we knew all along Dominic wasn't staying. Only visiting."

"But I thought—"

"You thought right," Dominic said from behind them.

Ireland gasped as Samuel scrambled up out of the swing and faced Dominic with his fists clenched at his sides. She reached for Samuel to pull him back to her, but her son evaded her touch and glared at Dominic.

"You're not going to make her cry."

Her heart shattered at Samuel's protective fierceness, and tears flooded her eyes once more because of the love behind it. Her son faced the man who'd hurt them, however unintentionally, tears streaming down his face, and Ireland prayed for Samuel's future wife to be worthy of such a treasure.

"I sure hope I don't, Sammy. But I would like to talk to her. Alone. With your permission."

"Sammy, it's okay. Go to the pier house and get a drink for me. Please. Sammy? I'm okay." Ireland waited until Samuel had walked a ways away before she allowed herself to exhale. "Dominic—"

"You said you didn't want a long-distance relationship. I know it's not ideal, but I'd like to know if there's any chance I can change your mind."

Afraid to hope, she crossed her hands over her front and waited. "Go on."

A hint of a smile pulled at his lips, distracting her,

but Dominic apparently took it as a good sign and stepped toward her, not stopping until she smelled his cologne and inhaled deeper because she wanted to internalize everything about this moment.

"I care for you, Ireland. I've… fallen in love with you, and I'd like to think you feel the same for me, even though we haven't known each other long."

"Lisa—"

"Was smarter than both of us," he said, holding the slip of paper in his hand up for her to take. "She always had a knack for this kind of stuff. Maybe it's woman's intuition or she had some kind of divine providence… I don't know. But she *knew*."

Frowning, she unfolded the paper.

Dear Dominic,

Oh, my love. What a year you've no doubt experienced. I'm sorry for leaving you, but I hope I've made my passing easier by the little surprises I arranged to brighten those dark days. And I hope when you get this letter you're tired of mourning and ready to get on with your life. Ready to be happy and create a new beginning with someone else.

We loved so deeply it will be hard, I know, but you must realize sharing that kind of love means you have an abundance of love to give to someone else. In my heart, I know you've avoided dating, thinking it's too soon, but, my love, life is short and you shouldn't waste a moment of the life you have left. So right now, I want you to know it's okay. I want you to remember me often but stop mourning. I want you to find that someone and go on dates and remember what it's like to be in love again. That's my wish for you, Dominic. To love and be happy. The kids will understand. We've discussed it already. They know to give you space when you realize you're ready.

Now, my surprise vacation for you… Did you enjoy it? I hope so. And I hope you found Ireland as sweet and loving and charming as I did. Call me crazy, but I see you two together.

Ireland gasped and looked up at Dominic, unable to believe what she'd read. "She... *Seriously?*"

"Keep going."

Ireland pulled her gaze from Dominic's, her shock making the paper tremble.

Dominic, Ireland's been hurt so badly in her past, and she needs the love of a good man. And Samuel... Oh, how that child made me laugh! He needs a father, Dominic. He needs a good man in his life to help him reach his potential. So, when you read this letter, I'm praying Ireland is still single, and I suggest you ask her out on a date immediately if you haven't already.

But if she isn't available, I hope you'll take this note as my dying wish that you find your next true north. You need someone by your side, someone who sees you and truly loves you. Find her, Dominic, and don't settle for less out of loneliness. Do it for me. For the kids. But most of all, for you.

With all my love, for eternity, Lisa

Ireland released a shuddering breath and clamped her hand over her mouth, unable to believe the last two weeks had been a thought in Lisa's mind when she'd visited two years ago. Much less that she'd— "I can't... I just can't believe..."

"Me, either. But she's right. Ireland, it will take some time to sort things out with work, but I don't want things between us to end. I don't want to leave *you*. I don't know if you feel the same way, but if you do, would you reconsider so that we can see where this goes?"

Reconsider? She laughed and cried and nodded all at once. Surged out of the swing to wrap her arms around him and press her lips to his. She kissed him over and over again, the precious letter clutched in her hand.

Dominic held her tightly against him, lifted her up so that their mouths were even, and took control and deepened the kiss for a long moment before he let her up for air.

"Is that a yes?"

She sniffled and laughed, pressed her forehead to his, and locked gazes so that there was no question as to how she felt. "Yes," she whispered, voice choked with emotion. "It's definitely a *yes*."

Want to read more about the Cohen sisters? Check out this short excerpt from LATTES AND LULLABYES:

Cooper Bale stared at the blinking cursor with gritty eyes. One of the twins let loose an ear-splitting scream in the living room, and the sound shredded his nerve endings. His almost-four-year-old niece and nephew were in rare form today after a restless night, which had left their recently hired nanny, Michelle, juggling the twins like a circus performer.

He leaned back in his office chair and pressed his palms to his eyes, attempting to rub the grittiness away. He'd gotten up with the twins last night as well, but short of turning whichever twin he held away from him so they focused on Michelle, he hadn't been much help in the kid-soothing department. He believed when they looked at him they saw him as the man who took them away from their mother and grandmother, even though he knew at their age that kind of thinking was unlikely.

The crying stopped and he listened to the soft tones of Michelle singing to them, trying to get them to join her. He scrubbed his hands over his face and tried to focus again, but the sound of footsteps approaching his office door left him muttering under his breath. A soft knock sounded. "Come in."

"Hey," Michelle said, Bella on her hip. "Sorry to interrupt but I needed to separate them and… I thought you might be able to use this." She carried a large steaming mug toward him and set it on his desk by his arm.

"Thanks."

"My pleasure." Releasing the cup, she moved her hand to his wrist and gently squeezed. "I know your deadline is looming, but you can do this. No worries."

Cooper stared at the polished fingers lingering on his wrist and sucked in a breath. Uh… surely he was misreading things? He was eleven years her senior and her boss. But Michelle had been finding excuses to touch him more and more, brushing against him as she walked by, grasping his hand or arm as she spoke to him or transferred one of the twins to him to carry. She couldn't think there was a chance he'd—

His cell phone buzzed and he used the opportunity to extract himself. No doubt it was his client requesting an update. Again. As he shifted away from her in the office chair, his hand settled on the device and he swiped to answer without looking at the number. "Bale."

"Um, hello? Is this Rocco's family?"

"Yes. Yes, hang on a second, please." To Michelle, he said, "I have to take this. Shut the door on your way out?"

The beautiful nanny pinned a smile to her lips and shook her head.

"Of course. Let me know when you need a refill."

Michelle carried his niece out of the office, but there was no way to mistake the look she gave him as she locked gazes before slowly shutting the door behind them.

Cooper closed his eyes and sat back in his office chair. First the twins acting out, Michelle being…*friendly*, and now his dog? At this rate he'd never meet his deadline. "Sorry. I'm here. Rocco's escaped again?"

"I'm afraid so. He hasn't been a bother, but he's here, at London's Lattes on Third, and I, uh, close in about an hour."

"I'll come get him."

"Thank you. And just so you know, I don't mind his visits. Truly. He's such a good dog. He's been here before. I, um, called then, too?"

He closed his eyes with a grimace. That trip. His mother had wanted to see the ocean one last time before she passed, see where the twins would be living, growing up… Just before they were to leave Charlotte to travel to Carolina Cove, his girlfriend had given him the ultimatum of choosing between her and the life they'd planned—or adopting the twins because they had no one else capable of giving them the life a child deserves. A compromise didn't seem to be possible, so she'd walked—run—away as fast as she could. "Yeah. Sorry about not getting back with you. I was here for… Well, things were a little hectic."

"Oh, no problem. I just worry about Rocco being picked up by Animal Control or hit by a car making his way home."

"Yeah, me, too. I'm not sure how he's getting out of the yard, but I'll take another look at the fence. Give me ten minutes to come get him."

In the background, one of the twins took the crying to a whole other level. Bedtime could not come soon enough, and no doubt Michelle could use a little privacy and quiet time herself. Maybe *that* was why she kept seeking him out? Was it her way of asking for help? For him to step up more than he had? But that was why he'd hired her. To take care them so he could work and keep a roof over their heads. "Maybe fifteen," he said since there was no disguising the noise in the background. "Did you say coffee shop?"

Michelle had come highly recommended by friends of friends of friends who'd said she worked for an agency overseas for four years before deciding to return to the States. He'd considered himself lucky to snag her on such short notice, especially since she'd already stuck through the hard transitions of his mother dying and girlfriend leaving.

"Yes. London's Lattes." The woman gave him the exact address and Cooper eyed his laptop and then the clock on the wall. "Don't let Rocco leave. I'm only a block away. I'll be there as soon as I can."

Cooper pressed the button to end the call and gathered up his things. The woman said she closed in about an hour, but he could get a lot done in that amount of uninterrupted time.

Backpack ready, he left his office and found Michelle had both kids strapped into their high chairs, eating an assortment of banana slices, yogurt, and cheerios.

"Sorry about all of the noise. Harry grabbed a toy from her and Bella was having none of it."

Harry and Bella. His kid sister had named her children after Harry Potter and Bella from *Twilight*. Examples of the fantasy worlds she'd tried so hard to escape into in order to remove herself from the reality of her own life as an addict and child of an alcoholic.

Cooper nodded, though there wasn't much about the situation he understood. After the childhood he and Ashley had experienced, he'd planned on never having kids, and his current reality wasn't something he'd envisioned, though he felt compelled to do. And poor Rocco—another gift for his girlfriend to keep her company when he had to travel—had been left behind just like he had. "You'll be okay if I head out for a while?"

"We'll be fine." Michelle smiled confidently. "After a snack, dinner, and some playtime in the bath, it'll be bedtime. We're almost there."

Almost was a long way from *there*.

Cooper managed a tired smile at the kids staring at him with their tear-smeared and wary expressions. Almost four or not, he had to believe that to them he was just another man who'd appeared in their life out of nowhere. He also knew they'd learned the hard way to be wary, but he was just as stressed as they were to accept the new norm.

Cooper chose to steer clear of the duo, hoping to spare the nanny more turmoil if their emotions flared once more. "Rocco's escaped again. I'm going to pick him up and… try to get some work done for my deadline."

"I was afraid of that. He went racing out the doggie door when Bella finally left him alone."

"He's adjusting to the move and the changes like the rest of us. Right, guys?" Bella stared at him like he was a monster about to devour her, and she puckered her lip to cry because of it.

"No," the little girl stated firmly.

"You said it," Cooper said, winking at the little girl.

Michelle laughed as though he was a comedian and

flashed him another blinding smile, and Cooper lifted his hand in a silent goodbye.

Michelle had his cell if she needed him, but everyone in the room knew who was best at handling the twins. The twenty-two-year-old had the skills and know-how to deal with them, whereas he… wasn't sure what to do. Nothing made the twins happy for long. Short of being a human bouncy or handing them sippy cups, which they promptly threw in their upset, he was at a loss.

The five-minute walk to the coffee shop helped clear his head and eased the knot drawing his shoulders up to his ears. He'd used the sidewalks to get there, having to walk down the street to the main road, down a block, and back south to the address. But as he did so, Cooper realized Rocco probably crossed from their yard into their neighbors' property and headed between the structures to the building housing London's Lattes. As the crow flew—or dog traveled—the coffee shop was only two backyards away and easily accessible.

A low woof greeted Cooper as he entered the coffee shop, but it was the woman behind the counter that drew his immediate attention with her light brown hair and bright green eyes that pierced him from across the room.

"That's the first time I've heard him bark. You must be Rocco's dad? I'm London Cohen."

London. The name suited her. Regal. Unique. It matched the eclectic cuteness of the coffee shop that looked to be a mixture of coffee and sandwiches, ice cream, beach-and-coffee-themed souvenirs, and comfortable gathering spots he eyed with pathetic excitement. "Cooper Bale. Nice to meet you," he said, turning his attention back to her. He closed the distance between them and shook her outstretched hand. "Thanks for watching out for him."

"My pleasure. Like I said, Rocco's never a bother. In fact, I've always been curious as to how old he is?"

"Three."

"Oh."

Her frown deepened at his words, and he followed her gaze to where Rocco lay on the floor beside a little wiener dog.

"I would've guessed him to be older. Rocco comes in, lies down, and sleeps by Rosie like he's completely worn out."

Tired as he was after last night's scream-fest, Cooper sympathized with the dog. "He doesn't get a lot of time to himself at home. The twins rarely leave him be unless he manages to hide somewhere."

"Oooh, no wonder he's such a tired boy. How old are your twins?"

London had moved closer to the animals and now bent to pet Rocco's head. Cooper watched, drawn even deeper into the empty coffee shop because of the dog—and the woman. Still, he was unsettled as always by the mention of "his" twins. "Uhh, going on four. A boy and a girl."

"Oh, that's a lot of energy in little packages. And cool that they're twins. I'm a twin, too."

There were two of her? London Cohen wasn't hard to look at, and any red-blooded male would appreciate the sight of her dressed in white shorts and a simple black T-shirt with London's Lattes in silver script that looked like steam over a coffee mug on the back.

Cooper watched as London's thick braid fell over

one shoulder when she shifted her weight to combat Rocco's when he leaned against her legs. The sparkles on her flip-flops caught the light. She wore a ring with a little dangle on the middle red-polished toe of her right foot.

Cooper shifted his gaze back to her face, wondering how a toe ring and sparkling green eyes nearly had his tongue hanging out of his mouth like Rocco's. "Uhh, trust me, Rocco gets more sleep than I do at this point."

"Aww, well, I'm sure it'll get better. Just a phase, right? How about a coffee?" she asked. "Or maybe a protein ball to boost the energy level?"

Rocco lowered himself to the floor, head on his paws, and closed his eyes. A pretty good indicator that to leave meant carrying the seventy-pound animal out of there if he tried to make the dog leave before Rocco was ready. "Yeah, please. I have some work I need to get done, but I won't keep you past closing. I'll take a coffee, black."

Cooper noted London's gaze narrowed upon hearing his coffee selection.

"Sure thing. Grab a seat. I'll bring it right out."

CLICK THE LINK TO CONTINUE READING LATTES AND LULLABYES OR CHECK OUT MORE SERIES AND TITLES BELOW. HAPPY READING!

THE SEASIDE SISTERS SERIES:

THE LAST GOODBYE
LATTES AND LULLABYES
MAP OF DREAMS
WORTH THE RISK
LOST LOVE FOUND

Books Also Set in Carolina Cove

CAROLINA COVE SERIES:

- SEASCAPES AND VEGAS MISTAKES
- SEASHELLS AND WEDDING BELLS
- SEA GLASS AND SECOND CHANCES
- SEA BLUE AND LOVING YOU
- SEA VIEW AND SOMETHING NEW

MAKE ME A MATCH SERIES:

- ROMANCE RESET
- RULES OF ENGAGEMENT
- THE MATCHMAKER'S SECRET
- PERFECTLY MISMATCHED
- BY THE BOOK

THE SEASIDE SISTERS SERIES:

- THE LAST GOODBYE

- LATTES AND LULLABYES
- MAP OF DREAMS
- WORTH THE RISK
- LOST LOVE FOUND

Excerpt of Sea View and
Something New

Isn't it funny, she mused, how failure opens one's eyes to true fear?

Sophia Shipley studied the outdoor patio and its well-dressed guests, careful to keep her turbulent thoughts masked behind a ready smile that showed none of the terror coursing through her body like electricity.

She'd left Carolina Cove, North Carolina, for college at eighteen and been on the fast track to success ever since. High school valedictorian, class president, lacrosse captain, cheer captain, and more scholarships than she could count. Her streak continued throughout college and again once she'd joined the workforce, but standing here now, in this moment, weighted with secrets, her spiral into the depths of failure had yet to slow. She'd thought leaving Raleigh in shame was her rock bottom, but now that she was here she realized it was just the start. Her heart raced in her chest, her grip on the champagne glass in her hand turning painful.

Tessa and Bruce Holloway danced, the newlyweds beaming with love and happiness. Sophia's heart squeezed at the sight and loved the fact that, despite their divorce in the 1970s, the couple had found their way back to one another again. Tonight was all about them, as it rightly should be. Which is why she needed to focus on the happy couple and not on the stress making her pulse pound in her ears.

She took another sip of champagne and glanced around the gorgeously decorated patio. The wedding planner had outdone herself. Cheryl Dummit had offered up her gorgeously landscaped yard as the location for the reception, and it looked breathtaking with its soft twinkle lights, candles, and decor.

A gorgeous glittery-gold backdrop took up on side, the perfect spot for guests to perch on a lush cream velvet settee for photos. It was all just… wow. Sophia couldn't imagine pulling together all the little details for something like this, but then again, that's how Eliza Bellefonte-Hayes had earned her reputation as the best wedding planner in the area. Some even said the state and beyond.

"You seem pensive," a voice said from behind her. "Is everything all right, Sophia?"

Sophia turned and sucked in a silent gasp. Barbara Lancaster, business woman of the year too many years to count, stood nearby, a glass of champagne in her hand. "Barbara, hello. It's good to see you."

"You as well. I wondered if you'd…make it back for this event," the older woman said carefully.

Sophia felt the color drain from her face.

She knew. "Barbara, I'm not sure what you've heard but I can assure you, gossip is rarely accurate."

Barbara's gaze narrowed into a shrewd stare and she took a long sip from her glass, staring at Sophia over the rim the entire time. After a moment of silent contemplation and a swallow, Barbara spoke.

"So the rumors are false? You haven't… quit the finance business?"

Sophia battled the hot flush of mortification that threatened to turn her body into lava, and forced her lips into a semblance of a smile. "Well, I suppose they are true then. Yes, I've taken a step back from the industry."

"And your step back has nothing to do with Bernard Pitz?"

Sophia faltered, aware of the tightrope she walked. The non-disclosure agreement was quite specific in terms and one whiff of a breach could land her in jail. "Barbara, you of all people know how it is. The rat race is insane and… after watching my cousins and sister find their significant others, it occurred to me what kind of sacrifices I'd truly have to make and…I'm just no longer sure that's what I want."

Barbara's expression made it clear Sophia could talk until the sun came up but the woman knew the truth. And didn't buy an ounce of Sophia's version of it. "Look, Barbara, the financial community is relatively small and I can only imagine what you've heard but you've been a close family friend all of my life which is why I'm asking you to not say anything to anyone. My parents don't know the details of my resignation and I'd like to keep it that way."

"I understand. But I'll just say this. Thirty-two years ago I worked with Bernie on a project and he was a putz and lech even then—and I wasn't nearly as beautiful as you. I'm sorry it—whatever it was— happened. And that you had to take blame for it."

"Barbara…" Sophia's voice trailed off as she battled the sharp sting of tears. Once again, she forced a smile in response to Barbara's implication.

She could do this. She would do this. Her career in finance might be over for reasons beyond her control but considering the circumstances, however unfair, she'd hold her head high. She chose to look at it as an opportunity to begin anew. To find her second passion and succeed with it. It was all a matter of setting her mind to it. "Tell me— How are you doing? Mama said you might go with the Babes on a Girls' cruise."

Barbara's expression made it clear the change in topic was noted but thankfully the older woman allowed it.

"Perhaps. I haven't decided yet. Will you be in the area long? Perhaps we could have lunch?"

A huff left Sophia's lungs before she could stop it. Literally no one in her family knew of her job loss or situation, yet Barbara had hit on everything Sophia had tried to avoid discussing the evening after her arrival. "I will be, actually. I signed a short-term lease today."

"Here? In Carolina Cove?"

"Yes. My family doesn't know yet," Sophia said, lowering her voice to give weight to the need for privacy. "So again, please, don't mention it?"

If Sophia hadn't known Barbara most of her life she wouldn't have trusted the other woman with the information but it was only a matter of time before she had to come clean with her parents. "It was spur of the moment and I'd like a few days or a week to myself before having to take on everyone's questions. Plus with all of the wedding preparations I didn't want my news to take any of the spotlight away from Tessa. I'm sure you understand."

"That's sweet of you, dear. Though I'm sure Tessa would understand your family's excitement that you're back in town. The Babes must be thrilled."

During the summers of '58 and '59, four of the prominent Carolina Cove neighbors and friends had given birth to baby girls.

The proud mamas had taken the five girls for daily strolls in their prams—and the locals had nicknamed the group the Boardwalk Babes—a name used to this day by the sixty-somethings.

"Though I do wonder how you think you're going to stay in the area under their noses for any length of time and not be discovered," Barbara said.

Sophia laughed and downed the last of her glass before exchanging it for another. "It may be a pipe dream but I'll take whatever time I can get."

"Rest assured your secrets are safe, my dear. It's been lovely talking to you and I do hope you'll be in touch regarding that lunch."

"Of course," Sophia said. "Maybe after I'm… settled." Barbara was sharp as a tack and maybe by then Sophia would have some business ideas to run by her and get her thoughts on.

"Yes, well, I'm going to go say my goodbyes. I have work to do before bed. Oh, I do envy you right now," the woman added. "I can't imagine having free time to sit and ponder life's possibilities."

Sophia forced a light laugh but it held no humor. She watched as Barbara walked away and took a fortifying sip.

Barbara had touched on every secret Sophia carried

due to stupidly trusting the wrong individual. And even though she had no one to blame but herself, the thought of starting from scratch scared her to no end. What if she couldn't do it?

"Rumor has it you're out of the game," a deep male voice said. "Yet here you are schmoozing. Looks like the spoiled rich girl didn't learn her lesson."

THAT WAS AN EXCERPT FROM SEA VIEW AND SOMETHING NEW AVAILABLE FOR PRE-ORDER NOW!

SEA VIEW AND SOMETHING NEW

Excerpt of Small Town Scandal

PAIN SURROUNDED her pregnant stomach and sharpened with knifelike intensity. Darcy Rhodes swallowed once, twice, as the threat of hurling abated along with the cramp that had taken her so by surprise.

Sliding into the narrow, Tennessee mountain road's salt-rusted guardrail hadn't been fun, but at least she'd stopped with a fairly light, if jarring, jolt. For a split second mid-skid, she'd wondered if she would plunge right over the edge.

You just had to keep driving to make up for the pee stops, didn't you?

She collapsed against her Volkswagen's seat, barely daring to breathe for fear that the pain would return or, worse, the movement would cause the guardrail to break and send her hurtling down the mountainside. Before the cramp had hit she'd done little more than reassure herself that she hadn't been severely injured—all body parts were still attached—and all four wheels appeared to be on solid, if slippery, ground. But now...

Now what?

The passenger-side air bag had deployed on impact and sagged across the dash like a deflated balloon. Chalky powder filled the air, making her nose itch and her throat burn. Who *wouldn't* tense up and react to what had happened?

She took a deep, cleansing breath, coughing weakly because of the powder. The cramp was just that, a mixture of fright and the need to pee. A normal reaction. As soon as she twisted the keys in the ignition the car would start and she would be on her way once again, slowly but surely. The very first hotel she saw, no matter how dirty, smelly or disgusting, she would stop without a single complaint.

The steady stream of freezing rain quickly changed over to a sleet-snow mix, and she watched, dazed, while the little bits of ice globbed together on her windshield before slowly sliding toward the hood.

Ignoring the weather as best she could, Darcy grasped the keys and turned. Nothing. Not even a stutter. She tried again. And again. *Nothing?*

She stared out the moisture-blurred windshield, her mind too full to think clearly. Mostly because it flashed to the horror flicks she'd watched as a kid. She knew what happened to stranded motorists—they were always the first victims. Back then she'd clamped her hands over her eyes to escape the scary parts, but there was no escaping this. When had she last seen a car? Twenty minutes? Half an hour? "They had better sense and stopped somewhere."

And now you're talking to yourself. Someone will be along soon.

But when? Darcy groaned, all too aware the passenger door was a lot closer than it had been five minutes ago, and shifted to find her cell phone. When she couldn't, she leaned over to peer into the dim abyss of the passenger floor, the shadow she cast negating the illumination offered by the overhead light. At least her air bag hadn't deployed and she hadn't hit the console between the seats. If she had, she could've broken a rib, and her baby—

Not going to go there, she told herself firmly. "Everything is fine." Her thick coat and the pillow she used for comfort had cushioned the impact.

Finally spotting the phone lying near an empty sour-cream-and-onion chips bag, she managed to snag it, only to swear at the illuminated display. She shook the phone, held it up in various spots in the interior of the car, but the little bars indicating signal strength didn't budge.

Her mind chose that moment to flash on an image of the movie heroine having car trouble and a strange man appearing out of nowhere and offering to help, the bowie knife concealed until it's too late.

Stop it!

Darcy turned off the overhead light and stared out at the landscape revealed by her one remaining headlight. At least the battery still worked. It didn't power the heat, but she wouldn't have to sit in total darkness while her mind ran amok.

Cold seeped into the car with every gusty blow of wind, the battered little Bug rocking with the force. *And when the bough breaks?*

"Nothing's going to break. You're not going to—"

Something struck the rear, the *thump* startling her so badly her breath hitched in her throat. What was *that?*

She jerked around to look out the back window, the

side mirrors, but saw nothing. The wind in the trees? A twig or branch? The road was littered with them, the combination of the wind and precipitation wreaking havoc on the area. Just her luck, she would have to get lost in the stupid forest.

Darcy double-checked the locks on the doors. If she jumped and tensed at every little sound, she'd be a basket case in no time. Maybe music would help? She turned the knob.

"And now a weather update…" Two seconds after finding a station, she groaned. In typical weatherman style, they'd gotten it wrong. The forecasted dusting of snow was now a full-fledged winter-storm advisory, and she was right in the middle of it with a car that wouldn't start and no cell service.

Where *was* everyone? Surely there was someone out on the roads. "Where's a cop when you actually need one?" She shoved her hair behind her ear, but it sprang right back.

"Be prepared for the worst," the too-chipper radio voice added. "We're in for a doozy. Stay indoors and conserve heat. Power outages are being reported throughout the listening area, and repair crews are running behind. For further updates and information, stay tuned. Up next is everyone's favorite, 'Don't worry, be happy.'"

Darcy rolled her eyes and turned the radio off with an angry twist of the knob. This couldn't be happening. Seriously, how many people got stuck like this?

Bands of muscle began to contract, up her back and around her middle. No, no, no. This was not happening. It was too soon.

She fought the pain, tensing, then just as quickly

tried to will the muscles lax. She was fine. *They* were fine. It was only a cramp. The phone in one hand, she rubbed her belly, noted that it was hard as a rock and getting harder, the ache in her back growing sharper and more uncomfortable. "It's just a cramp," she whispered, eyes squeezed tight. Slow, deep breaths. In and out. Calm. Soothing. She gave massages for a living, she knew soothing. She could *do* soothing. It was mind over matter.

"Just calm down. A car w-will be along soon, and this—" she exhaled, blowing the air out of her mouth "—is just a cramp…. Just an itsy-bitsy cra—*Ohhh!*"

The phone clattered as it hit the floor. Her hands fumbled, finally latching on to the steering wheel. She squeezed hard, a low moan escaping her lips she couldn't have held back if her life depended on it.

Finally the contraction—oh, God help her, they really *were* contractions!—subsided and that's when pure, unadulterated fear kicked in. No cell signal. Lost because of a wrong turn, stranded in the mountains in a snowstorm and—*in labor?*

"Oh, God, please. It's been a while. Okay, I know, it's been a long, *long* time, but please—" She bit her lip, unable to deny the truth any longer. "Help me. I can't do this here. I can't do this *alone*. I need help. *Please*, I need help!"

Time passed, minutes blurring together as contractions came and went. She remained where she was, her grip tight on the wheel, eyes closed during the worst of the pain when it felt as though her body was being shredded from back to front. Oh, please. Please, please, ple—

Bang-bang-bang!

The pounding on Darcy's car roof scared her so badly she shrieked and leaned sideways in the bucket seat to escape. How had she missed seeing the headlights of the vehicle stopped beside her car?

I've told you a million times, child. Ask and ye shall receive. Believe and, if it's His will, you'll be just fine.

She blinked, dazed by the combination of pain, surprise and the memory of her grandmother's voice.

"Hey," a man's voice called, "you okay in there?" *Bang, bang.* "Need some help?"

"Please don't let him have a knife." Her pain-tensed body tightened even more when she spied the large shadow looming outside her window. But what choice did she have?

Hoping Nana was right, Darcy flipped the lock, fumbled with the handle and pushed weakly, but the door didn't budge. She hit it with her palm.

Apparently catching on that the door wasn't opening, the man yanked twice before it gave with a shattering explosion of ice. "Are you all right?"

Unable to respond because the contraction hit its peak, she bit her lip and shook her head because it was all she could manage.

"Are you hurt?" The man's tone was more insistent.

She reached out and grabbed his overcoat to make sure he didn't leave and the soft, expensive feel of the cloth registered at the same time the banded muscles finally loosened their grip on her body. She fell against her seat in relief.

The man bent into the car, effectively blocking the opening and shielding her from the worst of the weather. She caught a brief sniff of his cologne. The dome light above their heads didn't illuminate much, but she was able to make out dark, close-trimmed hair, thick brows, a longish nose and the shaded roughness of lightly stubbled cheeks. He had to be gorgeous, didn't he?

His lips were turned down at the corners in a concentrated scowl, his expression clearly worried and concerned rather than threatening. A little of her anxiety eased, but not all. *If you sent me an angel, Nana, this one has black wings.*

"Where do you hurt?"

"I…I'm p-p—Oh, no." She moaned when another contraction made itself known, and vaguely heard her handsome rescuer mutter something indistinguishable when he realized the lump between her and the steering wheel wasn't just the bulk of her coat.

"You're *pregnant?*"

She managed a nod, imagining she heard his deep voice squeak a bit there at the end.

"Okay, uh—How far apart are the contractions?"

This pain ended fairly quickly and wasn't as intense as before. That was a good thing. Right? She released the air from her lungs in a gush. "They're…c-close together b-but irregular."

A glove-warmed hand brushed the hair off her forehead. He had calluses on his fingers, not thick or abrasive but there; something she wouldn't have guessed him to have, given his expensive appearance.

"How far along are you? Any special conditions? Who's your doctor?"

She struggled to focus on the questions. "I…I don't have a doctor. Not here. I'm on my way to Indiana." Her grip tightened on his coat. "I *can't* have the baby *here!"* She felt herself weakening, the fear she'd barely managed to keep locked away breaking free.

"Hey, no tears. Come on, sweetheart, don't do that to me," the man murmured. He brushed his thumb over her cheek.

The gesture had a calming effect, and even though her body ached and everything had gone wrong, she felt a connection with him.

Because he's the only thing standing between you and self-delivery. Did you even look for a knife?

"Stay still, okay? I'll go call for help. Don't move."

Like she could go anywhere else. The guy straightened and the door closed sharply, carried by the wind. The slam caused more ice to crack, and a small sheet slid down the windshield where it wedged beneath the wiper blade, obliterating her ability to see.

This was what it was like to suffocate. To feel hemmed in and confined, surrounded by darkness.

Melodramatic much? Just stay calm. All she had to do was keep it together and ignore the pain spreading along her back. Relax. *Breathe.* But what if the man didn't return? What if he went back to his car and drove away because he didn't want the responsibility of helping her? How many people *would* help her? Had it been someone else by the side of the road and her driving by, would she have stopped?

She gripped the steering wheel so tightly her fingers went numb. Then, as fast as it had come on her, the contraction ended, the tension subsiding to a dull ache.

Darcy huddled in her seat, cold in a hot and shivery, this-really-can't-be-happening kind of way. The baby would be fine. She had to believe that. She couldn't believe anything else because if she did—

She caught a glimpse of movement in her peripheral vision, unable to believe what she was seeing. The man's vehicle was *moving*.

Darcy straightened in the seat, her heart racing out of control the way it had when she'd been the new kid on the merry-go-round the bullies had tried to sling off. She flattened her hands on the window. Pounded on the glass. Her sweaty palms left prints behind. "Wait! Wait, don't leave!"

But the large vehicle drove on.

Images came again. First Stephen, his parents, the storm and the accident. The baby and now this. She dropped her forehead to the cold glass, fighting the cramping sensation as long as she could.

I asked, Nana. I asked! What now?

The contraction leaped from cramp status to uncomfortable, this-really-hurts *pain*. What now?

All she wanted was to give her baby the best life possible, make up for screwing up the beginning of its life. A nice home, someplace safe. Maybe a nice guy somewhere down the line. To *be* the mother—

You don't know how to be?

She wrapped her arms around her stomach and rocked. "*Please*…don't leave me."

KEEP READING SMALL TOWN SCANDAL: TAMING THE TULANES SERIES:

- SMALL TOWN SCANDAL
- THEIR SECRET BARGAIN
- CROSSING THE LINE
- THE NANNY'S SECRET
- SOMEONE TO TRUST

Also by Kay Lyons

MONTANA SECRETS SERIES:

- HEALING HER COWBOY
- IT HAD TO BE YOU
- HERS TO KEEP
- MILLION DOLLAR STANDOFF
- HIS CHRISTMAS WISH
- THEIR SECRET SON

THE SEASIDE SISTERS SERIES:

- THE LAST GOODBYE
- LATTES AND LULLABYES
- MAP OF DREAMS
- WORTH THE RISK
- LOST LOVE FOUND

TAMING THE TULANES SERIES:

- SMALL TOWN SCANDAL
- THEIR SECRET BARGAIN
- CROSSING THE LINE
- THE NANNY'S SECRET
- SOMEONE TO TRUST

THE STONE RIVER SERIES:

- WORTH THE WAIT

- NOT BY SIGHT
- THROUGH THE VALLEY
- LEAD ME NOT
- CHRISTMAS AT HOLLY WOOD
- THEIR CHRISTMAS MIRACLE
- SECOND CHANCES

SMALL TOWN SCANDALS SERIES:

- BRODY'S REDEMPTION
- FALLING FOR HER BOSS
- WITH THIS MAN

SECRET SANTA SERIES:

- SECRET SANTA
- SECRET SANTA II: A CHRISTMAS TO REMEMBER

MAKE ME A MATCH SERIES:

- ROMANCE RESET
- RULES OF ENGAGEMENT
- THE MATCHMAKER'S SECRET
- PERFECTLY MISMATCHED
- BY THE BOOK

CAROLINA COVE SERIES:

- SEASCAPES AND VEGAS MISTAKES
- SEASHELLS AND WEDDING BELLS
- SEA GLASS AND SECOND CHANCES
- SEA BLUE AND LOVING YOU

• SEA VIEW AND SOMETHING NEW

About the Author

Kay Lyons always wanted to be a writer, ever since the age of seven or eight when she copied the pictures out of a Charlie Brown book and rewrote the story because she didn't like the plot. Through the years her stories have changed but one characteristic stayed true— they were all romances. Each and every one of her manuscripts included a love story.

Published in 2005 with Harlequin Enterprises, Kay's first release was a national bestseller. Kay has also been a HOLT Medallion, Book Buyers Best and RITA Award nominee. Look for her most recent novels with Kindred Spirits Publishing.

For more information regarding her work, please visit Kay at the following:

www.kaylyonsauthor.com

@KayLyonsAuthor (Twitter)

Kay Lyons Author (Facebook)

Author_Kay_Lyons (Instagram)

Kay Lyons, Author (Pinterest)

SIGN UP FOR KAY'S NEWSLETTER AND RECEIVE UPDATES ON NEW RELEASES, CONTESTS, PRE-RELEASE BOOK INFORMATION, EXCLUSIVES AND MORE!